THE EVERYBODY EXPERIMENT

LISA MOORE RAMÉE

HARPER
An Imprint of HarperCollins*Publishers*

The Everybody Experiment

For information address HarperCollins Children's Books, a division of HarperCollins Publishers, 195 Broadway, New York, NY 10007.
www.harpercollinschildrens.com

Library of Congress Control Number: 2023944487
ISBN 978-0-06-303947-6

Typography by David DeWitt
24 25 26 27 28 LBC 5 4 3 2 1
First Edition

For the worriers and the criers and the ones who keep a fountain of emotion buried deep.
I see you.

"You ought to be ashamed of yourself," said Alice, "a great girl like you . . . to go on crying in this way! Stop this moment, I tell you!"
—*Alice's Adventures in Wonderland*, Lewis Carroll

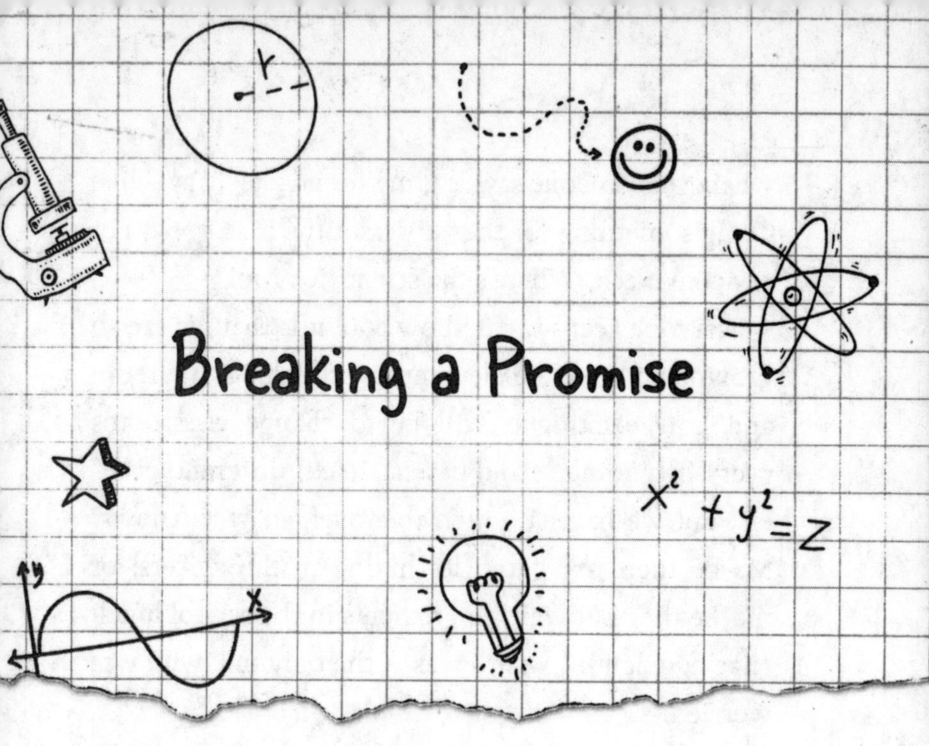

Breaking a Promise

Recess is my favorite part of the day. Twenty whole minutes of freedom—and me and my friends always make the most of it.

"Let's grab a rope," Naomi says as we head out of class. "This is our last recess. We gotta jump!"

Her reminder that this is the last time we will ever jump rope on the Bay View Elementary playground makes my stomach feel like it turned into a blender, swirling and whirling my insides all around. But none of my friends seem bothered. This final week of school has been about doing all the things we loved to do at Bay View. "A last hurrah," Mara called it. Lately, whenever someone says *last*, my friends say "Yay!" like doing something for the very last time is so great. I'm not convinced. Where's the scientific proof?

Everyone keeps saying how cool it is that we are so grown and won't be elementary school kids anymore and how exciting it will be to change classrooms every fifty minutes and have six (six!) different teachers. But we haven't gotten there yet, so who knows? Maybe there are gargoyles hiding in the lockers, or maybe they put weird ingredients in the school lunch (like eggplant). I wish I wasn't the only one who was worried.

Mara grabs the rainbow jump rope, which is our favorite, and wraps it a bunch of times around her waist like a belt. Then she does a little swivel with her hips and pumps her fist into the air and my worry gets gobbled up by giggles. Mara is good at cracking me up.

We make our way to our spot on the playground and Naomi takes one end of the rope and Mara takes the other. Nikila jumps in but I lean forward and back and forward and back feeling the tingle of kitten paws kneading my belly. Finally, I jump in too.

We have been jumping rope at recess since third grade. Back then, we would do Miss Mary Mack and Mabel, Mabel. But then last summer Naomi visited her cousins, and when she came back, she taught us all their rhymes.

"Down, down, baby, down by the roller coaster," Naomi and Mara sing together as Nikila and I jump side by side. We turn our backs to each other and then face each other and do our special hand claps. Then I jump out and stand next to Mara and she slides the end of the rope into my hand while it's still spinning, and I keep the rhythm going and Mara jumps in with Nikila.

"Shimmy, shimmy cocoa puff, shake it for me *now*!" Naomi sings at the top of her lungs.

Mara and Nikila both shake it. "It" is their bottoms, and they both shake so hard, Mara's glasses fly off and Nikila loses the rhythm. The rope slaps her ankle.

"Nik!" I shout. We've been trying to make it through an entire recess without a miss and this was our last chance.

"Sorry," Nikila says. "But my legs are all jiggly." She starts walking around like she's made of wet noodles and I can't be mad after that.

Mara grabs her glasses and puts them back on. "Should we try again?" she asks.

"No, let's do monkey bars before the bell rings," Naomi answers, and no one argues because although jumping rope is our favorite thing, monkey bars is a close second. It will be hard to say goodbye to them.

We take turns crossing the bright blue metal rungs and swing our legs and shout how we're bosses of the bars. We're the bosses now, but next year, we'll be back at the bottom. I get a little nervous if I think about it too much.

Naomi climbs up on top of the bars and stands there fearlessly. "Who wants to see me do a cherry bomb?" she asks.

Nikila raises her hand and waves it around frantically like we are in class and the teacher asked a question she knows the answer to.

"You can do one?" Mara asks suspiciously.

Cherry bombs take a lot of guts. You dangle from the bars by your knees and then swing yourself off, landing on your feet. But all four of us have been worried that what will really happen is we will land on our face, so none of us have tried it.

Instead of answering Mara, Naomi squats so that she is sitting on top of the bars. I think she looks nervous, but she doesn't hesitate to flip upside down so she's dangling by her knees and as soon as she does, her T-shirt slides up.

"You're wearing a bra!" I squeal in surprise.

Naomi grabs the bar again, unhooks her knees, and drops to the ground. "Kylie!" She tugs her shirt down and frowns at me.

"What?" I ask, and inside I'm thinking, *Uh-oh, here we go again.*

"Everyone knows you're not supposed to say stuff like that," Mara says as if she's saying blue and yellow make green.

"Yeah," Nikila says.

And then they all look at me like I'm a big weirdo.

My nose gets tingly like there is a fuzzy caterpillar inside, and I blink fast. I made a promise to myself and I'm trying really hard to keep it.

Naomi, Mara, Nikila, and I have been friends since before we even started at Bay View. We all went to Little Tots Preschool together and our moms became friends, so that meant we became friends. Or maybe our moms noticed that we all liked playing at the magic sand station together and decided they should be friends too. That's what my dad calls a "chicken or the egg" question. Who knows which came first? But it doesn't even matter because we are best friends.

But lately, it feels like things are changing. Moments like this one when they're all looking at me like I'm a buttoned-wrong sweater.

I want to ask Naomi why she is even wearing a bra, because like me and Nikila, she doesn't need one. And so what if I asked about it? It's not like there are any boys around. I mean, even I know you don't talk about personal undergarments when big-boy ears are anywhere near you. Why didn't she just tell us she had started wearing one? Then I wouldn't have been so surprised.

My eyes start to water, and I swipe at them fast.

"You're not going to *cry*, are you?" Naomi asks.

When you're just about to get out of elementary school, you're not supposed to cry anymore. (Unless you get hit right in the face with a tetherball the way Brian McKoy did two weeks ago.)

I know this is a rule, but my eyes don't seem to have gotten the message. I shake my head no. I *promised* myself. NO tears.

"You know she can't help it," Mara says, and shrugs like it's no big deal. Then she glances over at Naomi and gives the tiniest head shake. Naomi sighs and Nikila gets a worried frown.

And suddenly I'm certain of something. They have all talked about this. About *me*.

"Just forget it," Naomi says.

The bell rings and we all race to get in line. Naomi's words bang around in my head. How am I supposed to forget that I'm way too close to breaking my promise?

Cutting Onions

Nobody wants to be a crybaby, especially when you're about to go to seventh grade. I really don't want to cry so much. I really *can't* keep crying so much. That's why I promised myself that I would stop. Especially since lately, my friends—especially Naomi—seem to think tears are a big problem.

As we walk into class, I whisper to Naomi, "I'm sorry."

"Me too," she whispers back.

I'm so relieved at hearing those words that I almost start to . . . ugh!

I do a big fake yawn so I can squinch my eyes shut because the tears want to rush right out and if I start blubbering in the middle of social studies, Naomi will probably take her apology back.

The thing about tears is you might cry when you're sad, but you might also cry when you're happy. Right now, I'm feeling both things at once. I'm really giving my hypothalamus a workout.

This year, I did my science project on crying. A good experiment starts with a question, and I had plenty of those:

1. Why do I cry so much?
2. Is there something *wrong* with someone who is a human water fountain?
3. If I find out why people cry, will it stop other kids from teasing me about crying?
4. Is there a way to stop crying *all* the time?

Of course, I couldn't actually ask any of those questions for my project, so I thought of a different question.

When Momma cuts onions, she puts another onion on top of her head so she won't cry. That gave me an idea for my official science project question.

Question: What is the best way to stop crying when cutting onions?

Then I looked up different theories and chose one.

Hypothesis: Getting an onion very cold is the best way to avoid crying.

It was a painful experiment, because I had to cut a lot of onions trying all sorts of things and to be honest, I cried no matter what I tried.

But I did learn a whole lot about tears and about different parts of the brain. I just didn't answer any of the questions I really wanted to, and when we put our trifold boards up in the multipurpose room, Tyson Wheeler made a big joke about mine and what a *perfect* topic it was for a big crybaby. Which made me cry hot emotional tears. Those are the ones you cry when your limbic system tells glands in your eyes they need to water up. The limbic system is the part of your brain that controls emotions and it has different pieces—like the hypothalamus. Some people's limbic systems are more sensitive. And there's nothing wrong with that. At least not *scientifically*.

But sometimes I feel as if there is something wrong with being sensitive. Maybe there is something wrong with *me*. And maybe my friends think so too. What will happen if they decide I'm too babyish to hang out with?

I can't face the newness and strangeness of middle school without my best friends by my side.

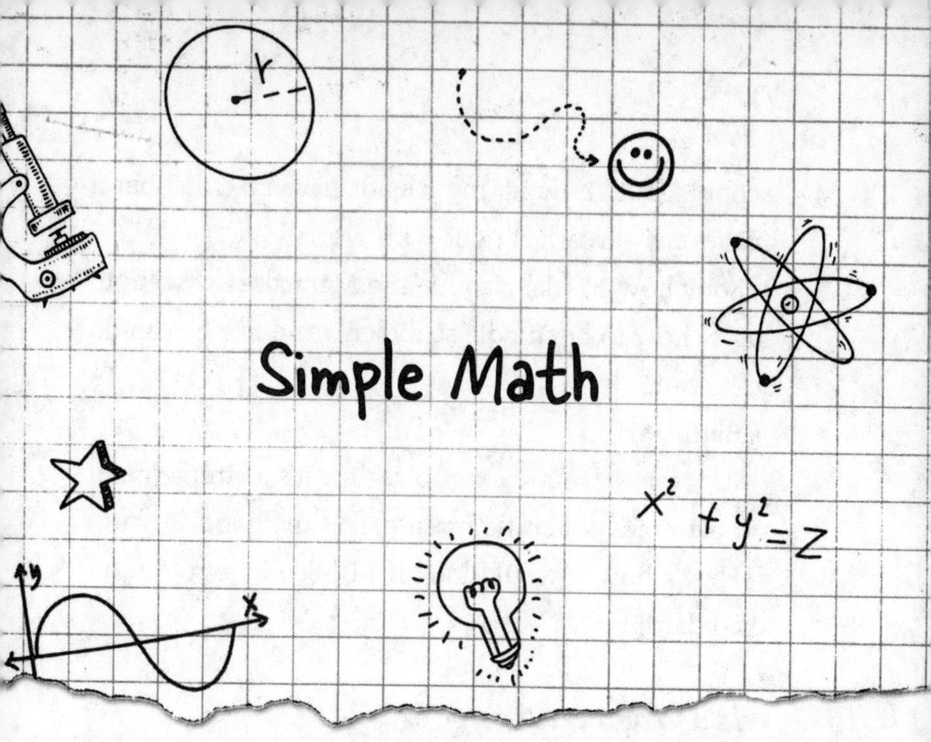

Simple Math

Even though my friends and I are in the same grade, I'm younger than all of them. Naomi's birthday is in November, so she turned six when we had almost just started kindergarten. Maybe that's why Naomi is so bossy.

Whenever Momma picks me up from school and notices I have red eyes (this has happened more times than I would like) she reminds me that I'm younger than my friends. That has never made me feel better. It sounds like she's calling me a baby.

Who wants a *baby* as a best friend?

I sure can't go around crying all the time in middle

school. And knowing my friends have talked about it makes my throat get tight with worry.

Somehow Nikila, Naomi, and Mara already seem to know how to be middle schoolers. And if they can do it, so can I.

But how?

It doesn't take me long to realize it's a simple math problem. My scientific brain makes me good at math.

Here's how it would look if Ms. Scobel wrote it on the board:

If a=b and c=a, then c=b

In other words, if my friends have already mastered how to be grown-up, then all I have to do is be just like them and I'll be grown-up too. That makes my friends = a; being grown-up = b; and me = c. If Ms. Scobel wrote that on the board it would look like this:

If friends (a) = grown-up (b), and Kylie (c) = friends (a), then Kylie (c) = grown-up (b)

I just have to equal my friends.

That shouldn't be hard. We like the same things. Like dance parties, games that we've invented that no one else knows, reading books with lots and lots of characters, getting good grades, and pineapple pizza. Still, it seems like they all got a book of instructions that I don't have. I'm really going to have to reflect on the problem.

That's what Momma says she's doing when I ask her something and she doesn't have an answer.

When Momma reflects on a problem it will usually take her only a few minutes before she snaps her fingers and nods. She also gets an expression on her face that makes it seem as if someone just told her they saved her the best piece of cake—the piece with a whole fat strawberry nestled in sweet cream.

Maybe her problems are simpler than mine.

I reflect on the problem for the rest of the day, but at last bell, when Ms. Scobel says "Okay class, it's official! You're done with sixth grade!" I still don't have an answer.

My classmates start chanting "Se-venth grade! Seventh grade!"

I don't chant. It will be hard to say goodbye to Ms. Scobel and reading club and Friday pizza. There's a big lump of tears in my chest, growing bigger like a storm cloud, but when Naomi gives me a look, I remember what I need to do, so I smile big to show I'm excited too. Naomi grins back and my tears fizzle away. Maybe the whole copying thing won't be *too* hard.

As we walk out of class, Nikila, Mara, Naomi, and I link arms and go all the way to the front of the school like that.

We're connected and doing exactly the same thing and it feels awesome, right up until I see Momma's car in the pickup line. My friends all started walking home this year. Momma says next year I can join the big group of kids who are allowed to walk instead of getting picked up from school.

I run to the car. "Momma, can I just walk home? Everybody else is."

"Don't be silly, Ky," Momma says. "I'm already here."

My little sister, Brianna, waves at me from the back seat but I ignore her.

"But—" I start.

"Kylie," Momma says in a warning voice, and I know better than to argue, so with a huff I climb in the car. After I buckle up, I sink low in my seat.

How can I copy my friends if Momma won't let me?

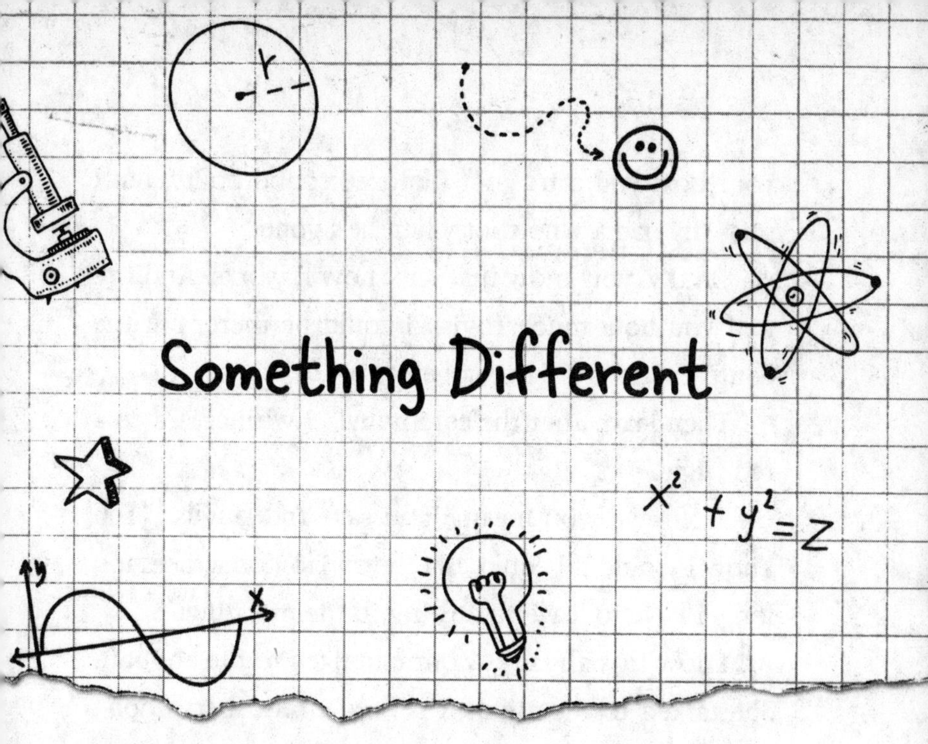

Something Different

Dad's big silver suitcase is on the bed, and he's neatly folding clothes while at the same time tossing a ball to Brianna. She is pretending to be a puppy and I'm not in the mood.

"But, Dad, you're going to miss my promotion," I complain. I am lying on the bed watching the pile of clothes that he's taking with him get higher and higher. That many clothes mean a really long trip. Maybe it's not too late for him to change his plans. Even though I knew he was leaving for a business trip, it still makes my heart feel small and brittle, as if a big deep breath will crack it in half. "Why can't you tell your boss you can't go?" I know I sound pouty, but I miss my dad a whole lot when he's gone.

"Oh, Ky, you know that's not how it works. And I've told you how much I wish I could be there, but the conference starts Saturday morning."

"Then leave after the ceremony!" I whine. "Catch a red flight."

"A red-eye, you mean," Dad says and laughs. "You know I would if I could. But the trip to Korea takes too long. I have to leave first thing in the morning."

I know this already. Momma talked to me about it. She talked to me about it several times. I still don't like it.

"Ruff! Ruff!" Brianna says. Then she starts panting really loud.

"Stop acting like a dog!" I tell her.

"Grrrr!" she growls at me, and I take off one of my socks and throw it at her.

"Kylie!" Momma says as she comes into the room. "I did not just see you throw something at your sister."

"It was a *sock*!" Obviously, a sock isn't going to hurt anyone. I don't know what the big deal is.

"I don't care what it was," Momma says. "We don't throw things at people in this house."

"Dad's been throwing a ball at her," I say.

"I've been throwing a ball *to* our little pup," Dad explains to Momma. Then he goes over and pets Brianna on the head and scratches her behind her ears and she makes little yippy noises.

I curl myself up small enough so that I could fit right into Dad's suitcase. Tears are filling up my eyes and any second, they'll spill over. I bury my face in my hands. "It won't be the same without you there," I say, but my voice is only a whisper and with my face covered, I'm sure no one hears me. That's probably a good thing. Momma asked me just yesterday to stop complaining about Dad's business trip.

"He *has* to go on this trip, Kylie," she told me. "And you're making him feel bad." I wanted to tell her how bad I felt, but then she added, "I need you to show how mature you are. I'm counting on you."

It was like a double-dog dare. Nobody wanted things to go back to the way they used to be.

Dad shakes my foot. "You'll be fine," he says. "Stantons are tough."

Brianna barks in agreement and I want to curl into an even tighter ball. Dad will be so disappointed in me if I keep acting like a baby. So will Momma. I have to prove I can be mature. What would my friends do?

I unfurl my body and force a smile on my face. "It's

okay, Dad," I say slowly, taking tiny breaths between each word. "I know you would be there if you could." I wish my friends were here to see how grown-up I'm acting.

"That's my girl," Dad says.

Momma smiles at me. "I knew you could handle it," she says.

Even though her words make me feel nervous, I sit up, wipe my face, and ask Brianna to fetch me my sock.

She bounds over to my sock, picks it up with her mouth (which is disgusting), and brings it over to me. She wags her bottom back and forth like a tail and I tell her she is a good dog.

"Yip! Yip!" Brianna shouts and licks my hand.

"Gross, Bree!" I tell her, but I can't help laughing.

But then Dad says, "You know, Ky, there's going to be a lot of changes ahead of you."

"I *know*, Dad," I say. This isn't the first time he has reminded me. Maybe what he's really saying is that I need to change because I don't seem ready for seventh grade. I know that too. But it's not as if I'm not trying.

Dad must see the worry on my face because he says, "Change can be scary, but remember"—he gives a shrug and then shuts his suitcase with a loud click—"all change is, is something different."

I gulp. Once Dad made rice with *raisins* and when I complained, he had said, "It's just something different."

Different sometimes means bad.

I think of my already mature best friends. We're different right now. But I'm going to figure out a way to be just like them.

An Answer

I wake up when my door creaks open, and I have two seconds to think it's a monster before Dad tiptoes over and gives me a kiss goodbye on my forehead. "Have the best day," he whispers. "I'll be back soon."

"Bye, Dad," I croak but he's already gone.

It's way too early for me to be up, but I can't get back to sleep. I'm too sad.

Dad got laid off a few years ago. I figure they call it being laid off because when it happens to you, you lie on the sofa a lot. And even though I hate that he travels now, when he was out of work it was a sad time for our family.

For almost a year, Dad laughed a lot less, and when he wasn't lying on the couch he was staring out the window or sitting at his computer muttering. Momma kept saying things like, "Everything's fine," and "I can always go back to work full-time," but nothing *felt* fine, and I didn't like to ask for school supplies or new shoes and stuff.

When Dad finally got a job, he told me he was going to have to travel a lot, but I was just happy to see him and Momma smiling again and for the big mound of worry to be shoveled away. I didn't know then how hard it was going to be with him gone almost all the time and how much I would miss him. Still, it's not like I can wish for him to be out of work again. And I want to be mature about him having to go.

But I don't feel like I can *handle* it like Momma said. What if when I'm onstage getting my certificate from Principal Lazar, I burst into tears because Dad isn't there? Momma will be disappointed in me, and my friends will be done with me for sure then. They'd be so embarrassed. So would I!

I *have* to start acting more grown-up. I know if I can be just like my friends, I'll be mature too, but I don't know *how* to be like them. Or how to get Momma to let me.

I flop over in frustration. "Ugh," I moan into my pillow. Figuring things out is supposed to be my thing. It's why I love the science fair. Every year I can't wait to decide on my project.

My walls are covered with all my science projects. One big trifold for each year. I love how you can ask almost any question and as long as you don't need to use dangerous chemicals in your research, you can find out an answer. (Even if it's not always the one you wanted.) But now I'm stuck. It's not as if *science* can solve my problem.

Wait. I sit straight up in bed. Why can't it?

Suddenly, all sorts of questions start buzzing around in my head. How can you be the same as someone? Can you *prove* that you're a grown-up? Is crying immature? What happens to seventh graders who cry all the time? *Are* there seventh graders who cry all the time?

The questions are like mosquitos biting me. No way can I go back to sleep now. I jump out of bed and turn on the light. I give my trifold with the details of my onion-and-tears experiment an appreciative fist bump, and then start reviewing the steps in my head.

When I think I have some solid ideas, I grab my supplies. Time to nail down exactly what I want to do.

After going through a heap of paper and totally

wasting my favorite gel magenta pen on several unworkable plans, I come up with a pretty good one. I'm excellent at writing out all the steps of an experiment because I have so much practice. You start with a question, and then you come up with your best guess for what the answer will be. That's called your hypothesis. Your hypothesis is based on research, so it's not *really* a guess. And to prove your hypothesis is right (or find out it's wrong) you do an experiment. The experiment is always the best part of the project. I want to prove I'm mature, and my experiment is going to do just that.

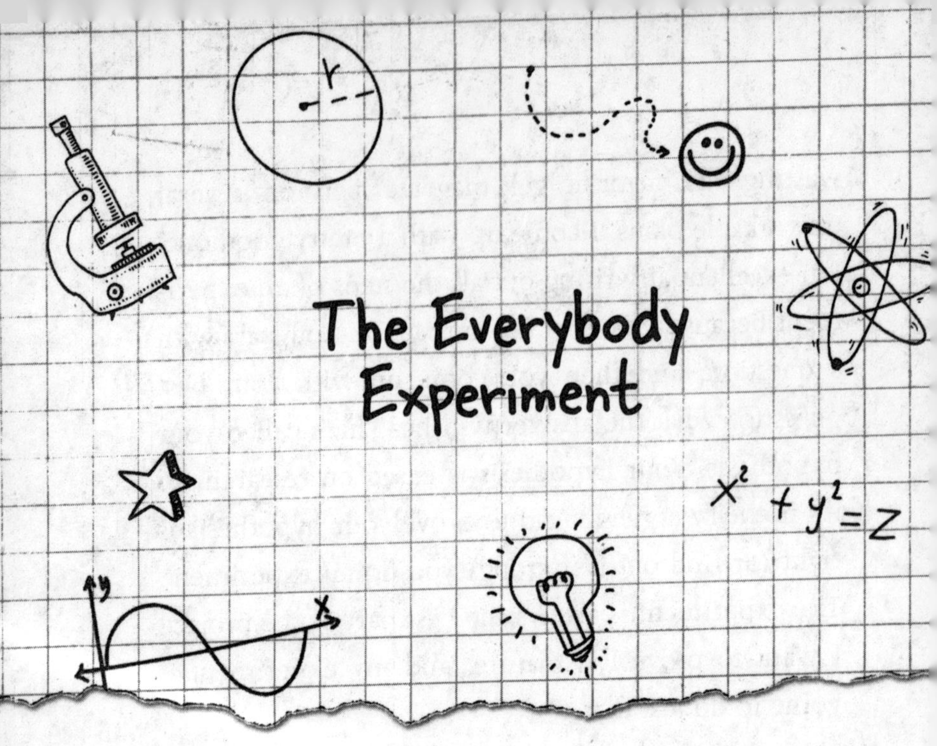

The Everybody Experiment

The sun is finally up and I can hear birds calling out to each other so I'm guessing it's not too early to hunt down Momma. The hardest part of my idea will be getting her to agree to it. After taking a deep breath, I tuck all my pages under my pj's top and head out of my room.

I find her in the kitchen having a cup of tea.

I get a banana off the island and start peeling it, considering the best strategy. "Morning, Momma."

Momma smiles at me with her relaxed morning face. Before Brianna has stepped all over her patience, or her phone blows up with texts and calls from her academic adviser.

I take a couple of bites of banana for sustenance and then I launch my attack.

"I'd like to test a theory," I say, trying to sound like a young scientist.

"What do you mean?" she asks, a little suspiciously.

"I have designed an experiment. A *science* experiment." I'm hoping that this will make her more likely to let me do it. Loving science is something we have in common. "In order to test maturity, I'll do everything my friends do this summer."

"I don't think so," Momma says without even taking a second to reflect on it. "That sounds like group thinking," she adds.

I know that in Momma's opinion, group thinking is bad news. Guess what? I don't care.

My dad's job is selling stuff, and he has to deal with people telling him no all the time. He told me once he has a strategy for turning a no into a yes. "I figure out what their obstacle is," he said. "Then I overcome it." I think I know the obstacle here. Momma's worried that group thinking will have me doing something that will get me hurt.

I look her in the eyes (another tip from my dad). "I won't do anything that will get me killed or maimed or horribly injured." I really don't want to get hurt; I just want to prove I'm grown-up and ready for seventh grade like my friends. "You always want me to have a project over the summer," I say. "This could be it! And you can make sure it is really sciency."

"*Sciency* isn't a word," Momma says.

I hold my breath, not sure if there's a no that's going to follow that.

She stares at me for a minute. "You need to write a clear plan," she says, and I almost tell her I already did, but she's not finished. "And if it adheres to the SCIENTIFIC METHOD"—she always says that like it's in all capitals—"and if it seems okay to me, I *might* let you try this experiment."

The way she says *experiment* makes it sound like she doesn't think very much of the idea, and with two *ifs* and one *might* in there, I'm a little nervous, but she hasn't said no and a small bud of hope is starting to bloom in my chest.

With a flourish, I whip out my stack of papers and hand them to Momma.

Her eyes widen in surprise, and she starts reading. I watch her lips move as she reads.

Question: Would a girl be mature if she does what everybody else does?

Research:

1. Last week when we were supposed to help the kindergartners with their end of the year water party, I had so much fun blowing bubbles and tying water balloons and splashing in the little kiddie pool . . . at first. I didn't know doing stuff like that is totally boring and that it is immature to enjoy things that little kids do. But my friends knew. All three of them spent the whole party leaning against the fence and looking annoyed and when Ms. Scobel reminded them we were all supposed to be helping they sighed and groaned like they were being tortured. If I had leaned against the fence with my friends, and moaned and sighed when forced to help, I would've been more like a middle schooler and acting grown-up. And I wouldn't have been embarrassed by looking so silly.
2. My friends know it's wrong to say if one of your friends is wearing a bra. Honestly, they know lots of things about being mature that I don't know yet.
3. Going into seventh grade is exciting and

everyone in my whole class is looking forward to it. And I should be too.

4. More than 60% of the time now, my friends say my name with a whole lot of exasperation. Saying Kylie like that is really saying, Don't you know how to be mature like us? (This statistic may be wrong; it may be more like 75%.)
5. It feels bad when I'm the only one who doesn't know how to act grown-up. I need to learn how to be mature so I will be prepared for seventh grade.
6. Friendships are important, especially as you get older and have to deal with lots and lots of things, so it is important to make sure you and your friends stick together.

Hypothesis: Kylie Stanton will be mature if she does the same thing as everybody else.

Experiment: This summer, when everyone does something, Kylie will do it too.

Results/Observations:

Conclusion:

Momma finishes reading and right off the bat, she asks, "How are you defining *mature*?"

I sigh heavily, but I don't want to be a sloppy scientist, so I take the pages back. I'm sure there is a way to explain maturity. I just have to figure it out.

Brianna walks into the kitchen and comes over to see what I'm working on. "Why are you doing homework? It's summer!"

"Leave me alone, Bree," I say.

"Kylie," Momma says and shakes her head.

No way can I get in trouble right now, so I say, "Brianna, *please* leave me alone."

Momma covers her mouth with her hand to hide her smile. Brianna starts making big loopy circles on a blank piece of paper and I go back to concentrating.

And almost immediately, I have the answer.

For the first time *ever*, me crying all the time could get me what I want.

A middle schooler needs to be less sniffly. I'm sure I can cry less! I think about the word *less* and how Momma will say it isn't precise. I need a specific number. To prove I'm grown-up like my friends I probably can't cry more than once a month. I can do that. Summer is three months long, so that means . . . I can cry only three times all summer.

Wow.

Saying it like that sounds really hard—especially

since I had been so close to tears only yesterday. But it is clearly *measurable*, which should satisfy Momma. If I'm right, I mean, if my hypothesis is correct, then I won't cry more than three times during my experiment. It makes me feel like someone put a boulder on my chest, but I amend my question.

"There's nothing wrong with crying," Momma says, and I don't even argue with her. She and I both know that crying as much as I do is a real problem.

"Okay, okay," she says, but before I can get all puffed up with pride at how cleverly I handled Momma's complaint, she lodges another one.

"Define *everybody*," she says, and my head lurches back in surprise.

Everybody is, everybody, right? Well, I don't mean the whole world, or even everybody in Alameda (where I live). It's who I mean when I want to go hang out at the park and Momma says "Well, who is going to be there?" and I say "*Everybody*, Momma." But I don't know how to explain that, so I decide my group of friends will work, because not only is it easy to list them, it's also really who I care about anyway.

To make my write-up look official I call me and my friends Group A.

Group A:
Naomi
Mara
Nikila
Kylie

So now I have:

Question: Would a girl be mature* if she does what everybody in Group A (see attached list) does?
*Mature = crying less than once a month

While Momma rereads the pages, I mentally add some details to Group A:

Naomi: short, skinny, but strong as a seat belt; big teaser; likes drama and making up stories

Nikila: super giggly; double piercing on both ears; fingernails chewed to the quick, but she's trying to stop; plays piano really good; easy-going

Mara: very tall—a kid once said "freakishly" tall and she punched him right in the stomach—she's the only one of us that needs a bra, and she started getting periods at the beginning of fifth grade; wears glasses;

loves sports but especially volleyball; will fight anyone who messes with us

Kylie: scientific; big poofy hair; brown belt in karate; *may* be too sensitive.

If I were to add a chart of how mature we all are, it would look like this:

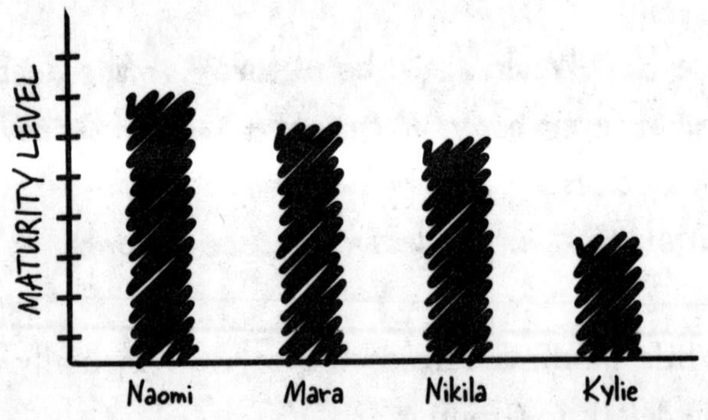

Momma gets flinty-eyed, which happens when she is getting worried about me. "You would actually do 'anything' everybody else is doing?" She puts little air quotes around *anything* and shakes her head.

This is her way of asking if I would jump off a bridge if everyone else did. And that's ridiculous. First off, none of my friends want to jump off a bridge. Second, of course I wouldn't jump if they did. But I add this:

Exclusions, prohibitions, etc.: Any behavior deemed "dangerous" or illegal will not be copied.

"How's that?" I ask hopefully. There's a little tickle in my chest as if a small bird is slowly beating its wings inside me. Momma just *has* to let me do this.

"I think *dangerous* could be more clearly defined," she says.

"Mo-omma!" I groan, because she and I both know what dangerous means. It's not as if she doesn't warn me every five seconds about the dangers of the internet and swimming pools and playing with sharp things, and on and on, so we're both real clear on dangerous activities.

She sighs all loud, but then nods.

Suddenly, without any prompting from Momma, I think of something I should add:

Additional information: Any crying associated with obvious physical pain (e.g., breaking a leg, falling while roller-skating and whacking your head really hard, getting the wind knocked out of you by an overly aggressive kickboxer, etc., etc.) will not be added to the cry count total.

Crying because you get *physically* hurt has nothing to do with what I'm trying to prove here. That should be obvious, but in an experiment, you want everything laid out nice and clear. Then I think of one more thing:

Happy tears also don't count.

I think I've covered everything.

"So?" I ask. "Can I do it?" I clasp my hands together.

Momma glances up and shakes her head, and I don't know what that means. Is she saying no? Should I have put in more examples of all the times I have gotten things wrong lately? Did I misspell hypothesis? She turns the pages over like she is checking to make sure I haven't written any secret stuff on the back, and then she shakes them like a tambourine.

"Kylie," she starts and then pauses.

She's wearing her reflecting-on-the-problem face. She is probably wondering whether this is one of those times when she should call my dad and get his "buy-in."

Momma having to get Dad's buy-in from far away can be a pain. With time differences and everything, sometimes I have to wait a whole *day* to get an answer.

Frowning, Momma says, "I'm going to say yes to this, even though I'm almost certain it isn't a good idea." Then she says, "You are going to have to learn some things the hard way, I suppose." She initials the bottom of the first page and hands the papers back to me. "Good luck."

"Thanks," I say, as if she was actually wishing me luck.

She looks at her watch. "You better start to get ready. Big day today!"

Brianna starts clapping like the big day is for *her* and I race to my room. My great experiment is about to begin!

Completely Wrong

When we get to Bay View, we don't have to go to our classrooms; we just head straight to the multipurpose room for the promotion ceremony. Younger kids are heading out to recess, except for the ones who have a big sister or brother who is getting promoted. I can hear the sounds of balls bouncing on the asphalt and shouts for being first in tetherball. I wish I could join the little kids, or better yet, I wish I could go pout in the car.

I can't believe I got it wrong *again*. And I can't even cry about it. I can't cry on the very first day of my experiment. As soon as I saw my friends I had asked

Momma if I could go back home to change. She rolled her eyes and shook her head like I was being ridiculous. I didn't feel ridiculous. I felt like a *baby*.

With all the talk lately about acting more grown-up and being ready for seventh grade, I had known I had to get my promotion outfit right. When Momma and I had gone shopping I had kept my eye out for something that screamed READY FOR SEVENTH GRADE! We found the perfect dress in the junior department and Momma got me shoes with heels on them. *Junior* department! *Heels!* How grown-up, right?

Not right.

All my friends wore new jeans and cute tops and had their hair down, swinging free. Nikila is Indian American and has dark brown hair that has only a tiny bit of a wave and looks like a river washing down her back. Mara is white and has straight blond hair that is all golden and shiny. Naomi is half Black and half Filipino and her hair used to be curly (but definitely not as poofy as mine), but now that she straightens it, it looks like a shiny black piece of glass. If I took my hair out of the two braids I wear on either side of my head, it would blow up like peacock feathers.

Melody Zacharias is also wearing a dress and that does not put me in any type of good company.

I guess I should have asked my friends what they were planning to wear, but how was I supposed to know I didn't even understand how to *dress* right?

The only thing that keeps me from crying is focusing on the delicious sushi lunch Mom promised we'd have after the ceremony.

My feet feel like they are being pinched by hermit crabs and ashiness has crept from my heels to my knees. I totally forgot to lotion like Momma told me. If you don't ever get ashy, you're probably not Black, but let me tell you, it's not a good look.

If my auntie Carrie was there, she'd ask, *Walked through a volcano?* Auntie Carrie thinks she's hilarious but she's not. But my legs do look like they are covered in ash instead of the shiny tops of chestnuts like they usually do. If I had worn pants today like my friends, no one would have seen my ashy legs.

When Principal Lazar calls my name to get my certificate, I tug at my dress to see if I can make it longer but it's no use and my nose starts to run. Uh-oh. I sniff a couple of times, and Naomi gives me a warning look and says, "Don't."

I want to tell her that I wasn't about to cry. But that might not be completely true.

After the ceremony, we all go outside and I try to

figure out how to walk in shoes that are biting me, while parents take a gazillion pictures.

We're in the small courtyard outside the multipurpose room and most everybody is whooping and hollering. You'd think they hated Bay View Elementary by how excited they all seem to leave it. Brett Matthews and Tony Silva chase each other around the bench next to the flagpole and not even Principal Lazar tells them to stop. If you ask me, chasing each other is pretty immature, but no one says they're acting young for their age. It's like people *expect* boys to be immature.

How is that fair?

Every time a camera is pointed my way, I step behind someone. Seagulls fly above our heads making a big racket and I'm pretty sure they're laughing at me.

Nikila's mom, Mrs. Kumar, says how mature we all look and then she tells me, "Oh, Kylie, you look so *precious.*"

Mara's brother, Mady, smirks at me. He's seventeen and quite the smirker. His baseball cap is pulled down almost covering his eyes and his big jeans are sitting too low. "Nice dress," he says.

That was not a compliment.

Mara jabs him with her elbow. Mara is a good

person to have on your side. She's tough. Momma calls her "steadfast." That means she's like the mussels that cling to the side of the pier at the beach. Just try to pry one off.

I try to smile at her but my feet throb. I think if I have to stand in these torture shoes much longer, my feet might have to be amputated. For the hundredth time, I wish Dad was here. He would say something silly and get me to laugh. My nose starts to tingle again and my eyes itch. I try thinking grown-up thoughts like recycling and gas prices and politics. A very small tear is in the corner of my left eye.

My sister, Brianna, is wearing a dress too, and she starts twirling around to make hers poof out. "Brianna!" I say.

She lurches over to me, all dizzy, and grabs my hands to keep from falling. I don't know why she would think I was calling her when obviously my tone was saying, *Stop what you are doing right now.*

"Act your age," I say, and she looks at me like I don't make any sense, because of course that's exactly what she is doing.

None of my friends have a little sister latched on to them. Nikila is holding her baby brother, Chetan, but that makes her look very grown-up. Her dad is taking pictures while my friends pose and Mara keeps tossing her hair back, like it's *such* an issue. Well, I can't copy any of that.

First off, I don't want my picture taken.

Second, as already stated, I don't have the type of hair Mara does.

And third, Dad can't take pictures from Korea.

I pry Brianna off me.

Then Mara's mom, Mrs. Wilson, says to Momma, "Laura, why don't we let the girls have a special grown-up lunch? I can drop them at Jack's and pick them up in an hour or so."

"Dutely, tutely!" Naomi crows.

This is our way of letting people know we are saying *absolutely* yes.

"You mean have them eat there by themselves?" Momma asks, not sounding enthusiastic at all.

My friends grin like it's the best idea ever, but I don't. Sushi is my favorite thing to eat. I have been looking forward to it all week because I know Momma will let me get the edamame appetizer, and miso soup, and tekka maki, *and* a supremely delicious dragon roll.

But if I'm going to copy my friends, I know I should be grinning like a quokka at the idea of eating alone at Jack's with no parental units. (Some people think hyenas are smiley, but I researched what animals smile when I was in fourth grade and quokkas are really the best.)

"I'll make sure they get seated and will be right next door at Michael's," Mrs. Wilson says.

Mara once had to fly to Seattle by herself, so I know Mrs. Wilson doesn't think eating lunch at Jack's without our parents is a big deal.

"Well," Momma says slowly. "We already had plans for lunch today." She is saying one thing, but her tone is saying something else. I'm sure she doesn't like this idea.

My friends look at me like I said something wrong, which is unfair since I didn't say anything, but I guess they think I'm *supposed* to say something.

"Momma!" I say, as if I actually want to miss out on sushi and eat a hamburger instead.

I give a small sneaky glance at Momma, ready for her to do what she usually does and say no. But this time, she looks at me, looks at my friends, and says, "Well, if you girls would rather have lunch together, that's fine."

"Okay, then," Mrs. Wilson says.

Welp, there goes my delicious sushi.

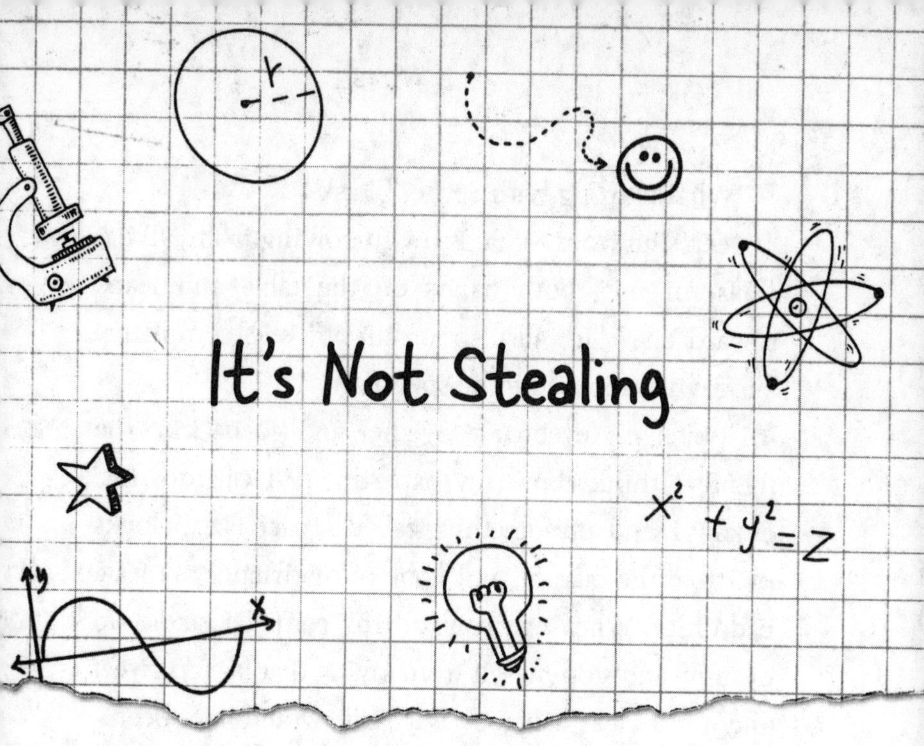

It's Not Stealing

When the waiter takes our order, Mara orders a Shirley Temple and Nikila says she'll have a white, frothy, coconut and pineapple concoction, and Naomi orders a raspberry lemonade that comes with a ribbon of red sugar spread on the rim of the glass. It's my turn to order. I have been paying attention to my friends so I can get something that says I'm just as ready for middle school as they are and so very, very cool. I know exactly what to get.

"I'd like a glass of Sprite, please," I say. This is quite bold of me, because my mom doesn't let me drink soda, but my friends groan and Naomi says, "Kylie!"

"What's wrong with Sprite?" I ask.

Deep sigh from Mara. Brow furrowing from Nikila.

Naomi puts both hands on the table and leans toward me. "It's just so ordinary," she complains. "Today is supposed to be special."

I pinch my eyebrows together and go back to the menu. I think about my experiment. I can do this. Finally, I settle on something called a Peach Fizz. It looks pretty in the picture, and none of my friends say it's a bad order. When everyone's drink comes, I take a sip of mine and stop myself from saying that it's too sweet and not at all as delicious as a Sprite would have been.

"Hey, you guys," Naomi whispers and we all bend closer. "You think our waitress is just a regular person, but she's really a princess from a faraway galaxy. She's leading a rebellion! She's going to put our bill in a top-secret folder so no one can see it's really the plans for the Empire's weapons."

Naomi loves to tell made-up stories about people. I look around to find our waitress and she does have an awful lot of earrings in her ears. And brightly colored hair. I could buy that she's from another planet.

Mara says, "You just stole the *Star Wars* story. You can't do that." Mara loves everything *Star Wars*, so she should know.

"It's not stealing," Naomi says. "It's a *retelling*." She huffs and then says that she got it wrong, that really our waitress is an alien assassin who has come to Earth to find the horrible beast who escaped from their world's prison. She is trying to blend in with Earthlings while she's hunting her prey, but doesn't realize orange eyeliner and wearing a ring on every finger and having hair that is as pink and poofy as cotton candy is a dead giveaway for alien.

Nikila snort laughs and it makes her white frothy drink shoot right out of her nose and all of us start laughing so hard that we have tears streaming out our eyes.

Suddenly my peach drink isn't all that bad. And everything seems exactly right.

When Mrs. Wilson drops me at home later, I go searching for Momma. It's a long shot but I think I might be able to convince her to take me out for sushi dinner. Maybe I can be grown-up *and* get a dragon roll.

But before I can ask Momma about going out for dinner, she says she's glad I got to have my celebratory meal because she has a "ton" of work to get caught up on. She has her computer on the kitchen table and a stack of books next to it.

"We'll order pizza," she says, trying to make it

sound special, but with Momma being so busy most days, we get pizza an awful lot.

To prove how mature I am I say, "That sounds great."

Momma has already bent back over her computer and I'm not sure if she even hears me.

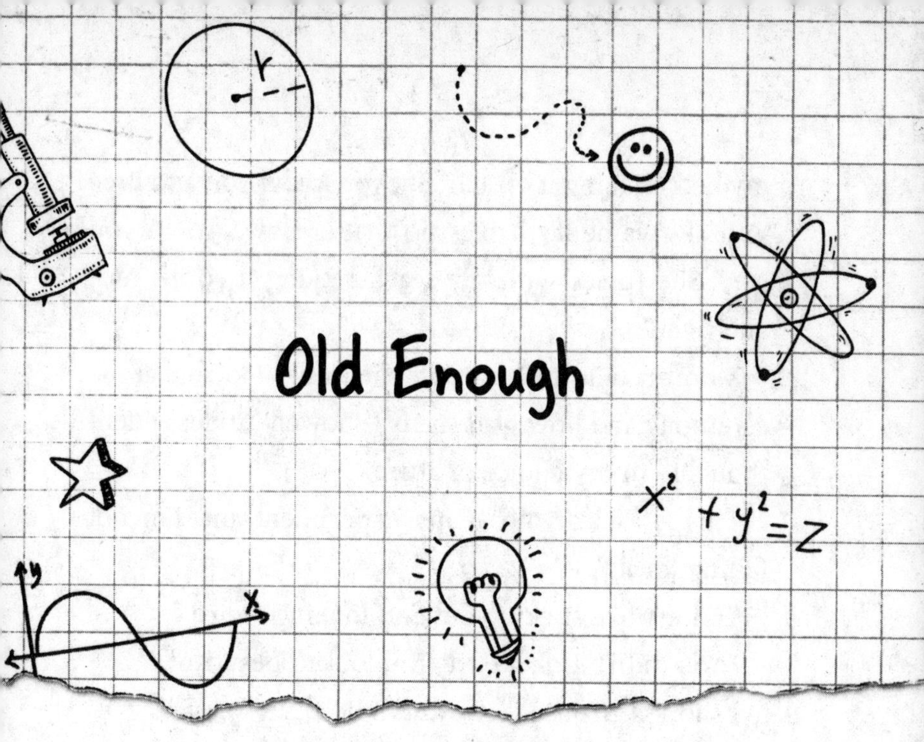

Old Enough

Later that night, after Momma reads Brianna a bedtime story, she comes into my room to check on me and say good night.

Her hair is wrapped up in a silky scarf just like mine and she yawns when she bends down to give me a kiss. "Good night, baby."

"I'm not a baby," I say and squish low into my too hot cotton sheets. They have chipmunks romping all over them and yesterday they were my favorite sheets, but tonight I realize they are for babies, and I do not like them at all.

"Of course not," Momma says and settles down on

my bed, making it creak. "But you know you and Bree will always be my babies no matter how grown you get." She fusses with my scarf, retying it so it's nice and tight.

Momma tells me how nice she thinks I looked at the ceremony and how glad she is I showed "independent thought" in my choice of attire.

This is a clear dig at my experiment and I'm not falling for it.

"I don't like sticking out and looking weird."

"You didn't look weird. You looked beautiful."

I snort at that. "I just want to do things *right*."

She nods, but then she says, "So did you like going out with your friends today, instead of getting sushi?"

I really cannot lie—especially not to Momma. It's physically impossible. If I try, I pause and stutter and my face gets red—which considering how brown-skinned I am, isn't so easy.

"I—I . . . had fun," I stutter. It's not a lie. It did feel grown-up to eat at a restaurant without our parents—but I also really wanted sushi.

Momma says, "It can be hard trying to figure out how to be at this age. Maybe that's why so many societies established cultural norms and rites of passage." Her voice gets a little dreamy. "That might be something to add to my dissertation." Momma talks like this a lot. She's working to get her PhD in anthropology, which means she spends all her time studying different people's backgrounds and cultures and stuff, and then writing long (really long) papers about them. One day she will be Dr. Stanton and we'll have a big party for her, and she will write even longer papers.

She's told me some stories about puberty rites in other cultures, and I'm sure they are supposed to make me feel lucky to be me (free to do whatever she'll let me) but it seems to me that it would be easier if everybody had to follow the same rules. Like in ancient Rome, the boys all wore togas with a red border when they were little, but when they got old enough, they wore all-white togas. A rule like that makes things so much easier.

Girls wouldn't show up to a ceremony thinking they were wearing the perfect dress that ends up being so completely unperfect.

"I guess," I say.

"So you still want to go forward with this experiment?"

I know she wants me to say I've changed my mind, and I almost tell her then that if I don't prove I'm mature, I am going to lose my friends. But I know if

I say that, she'll say something like friends like that aren't worth keeping, or something else silly. I *need* my friends. I am going to prove to them I'm just as mature as they are. "Yep," I say.

"Okay, Ky," Momma says. "Sweet dreams." She turns off the light and heads out of the room, but just before she leaves, she turns and asks me, "Do you want me to turn on the closet light?"

Momma knows me and dark aren't exactly best friends.

"No," I say, wishing I meant it.

Still Brand-New

The next day, I don't know what to do with myself. I'm ready to continue my experiment, but there's nothing going on. I wander into my room and look at myself in my daisy-shaped mirror. I try looking bored and grown-up but end up giggling instead. Then my phone buzzes.

It's a text from Naomi saying her mom can drop us off at Shoreline Mall, and do I want to go. The fact that Naomi is texting me is a super big deal because I just got a cell phone. My friends have had their phones since last year, but Momma and Dad said I was too young. But I did a good job arguing that now that I'll be walking to middle school—which is a lot more blocks away than elementary—I should really have a cell phone. For safety.

Momma and Dad didn't seem happy about it but gave me a cell phone last month for an early promotion-from-elementary-school present. It has a purple case with rhinestones, and I love it more than I love my baby sister.

Going to lunch by ourselves was one thing, but I don't know what Momma will think about us going to Shoreline. Shoreline is an outdoor mall and it doesn't have a lot of stores that my friends and I like, but when you live on Alameda Island, you don't have a lot of shopping options.

If you tell people you live on an island, they will imagine sandy beaches and palm trees and coconuts. Alameda isn't anything like that. It's just a regular place, with neighborhoods and streets and traffic lights. You do have to use a bridge to get to the rest of the Bay Area, but mostly we forget we even live on an island.

Is your mom going to stay with us? I text back.

No. She'll pick us up later. Can you go?

Nobody wants to plan sleepovers at my house because by midnight Momma has had enough with the noise and the mess and the demands for snacks and tells us it's time for bed. My friends' moms obviously got a different mother handbook because when

I sleep over at their houses, they just tell us not to be too loud and then they go to bed and don't care how late we stay up. Even Nikila's mom lets us stay up as late as we want and she's *almost* as strict as Momma.

I tap my phone, wondering. Then I click on a smiley face emoji.

Sure, I can go.

Don't you have to ask?

No.

I'm not really sure. Don't the parameters of my experiment mean that I don't have to ask?

Really?

Fine. I'll check.

This is the problem with science experiments. It's hard to make sure you've figured out every single solitary thing.

I find Momma in her office reading a book and taking notes. "Momma, my friends are hanging out at Shoreline, so I'm going to go too, okay?" (I had originally planned to leave off the "okay" at the end, but my experiment is still brand-new, so I'm sort of riding with training wheels.)

She doesn't even look up. "Anybody's mom going to be there?"

"No."

No noise except the sound of a page turning.

"I do have some things I need to get from the mall. Maybe I could—"

"Momma!"

More silence.

"Okay, Kylie."

Wow. First battle and no war wounds. I text Naomi.

I can go.

Really????????!!!!!!!!!

I don't think Naomi needs to use so many exclamation marks.

Dutely, Tutely.

We'll pick you up. See you in thirty! 😊❤

I run back to my room to get ready and realize right away I don't know what to wear. I definitely don't want a replay of yesterday. I also don't want to ask Naomi because I want to seem like I *know* how to be grown-up even if I don't. Maybe now that we are out of elementary school, we need to dress for the mall like the teenage girls who tromp around in their makeup and tiny tops and carry big rhinestone purses. I go to find Brianna. "Hey, Bree, you wanna do me a solid?" (Solids are what my friends and I call favors.)

"What do I have to do?" she asks, already suspicious.

"Easy peasy," I say. "Naomi is coming over. I want you to peek out the window when she gets out of the car and shout up to me 'plain' or 'fancy' when you see what she's wearing, okay?"

"Is there something wrong with your eyes? Did you try those droppie things again?"

Last year, I saw a commercial that made me really want to try eye drops. The model was singing about how she could see so clearly. I found a little plastic bottle in the medicine cabinet that looked just like the bottle on TV, so I put some drops in my eyes. This was a very bad idea. I did not smile like the model on television. My eyes burned like they were on fire and Brianna had worried I was going to be blind—I worried too. I blinked and blinked but the burning didn't stop.

"You know better!" Momma had said as she helped me rinse my grandmother's glaucoma medicine out of my eyes. She made me promise not to ever do something like that again. She didn't have to worry. I barely want to get my toothbrush out of the medicine cabinet now.

I shake my head at Brianna. "No, I didn't put drops in my eyes. I can see fine."

"Then why do you need me to tell you?" she asks in a loud whisper, as if there is something secret and magical underfoot. Brianna is completely in love with fantasy worlds, especially Sparkle World from the series of Sparkle Magic books. She always wants us to pretend we are the elf twins Luna and Lena. They have all sorts of fun and sometimes scary adventures. She keeps hoping she'll find an elf or fairy in our yard one day.

"I just do," I say. "So, like if she's wearing a dress, then yell 'fancy,' but if she's just in shorts and a tank, shout out, 'plain.' Got it?"

"But that's silly," Brianna says, sounding disappointed. "Won't you see what she's wearing when you answer the door?"

"I want to know before."

"Why?"

"I don't want to be fancy if she's plain and I don't want to be plain if she's fancy." I speak calmly even though I want to shout at her. It seems very simple to me. "Okay?"

"Why don't you just wear your giraffe pants?"

I have a pair of yellow flannel pants with brown spots I wear to sleep in and lounge around the house in, and Brianna believes they make me look like I have giraffe legs. They have pom-poms on the bottom and are a little ratty because I've had them a long time. Momma got them from the little girls' department, and they are a size 6X. They still fit me even though I'm way past six years old, and I love them. Brianna also loves the pants, and she has said if they were hers, she'd wear them all the time. But it is my sincere hope my friends never see me in these pants, as it would be hugely embarrassing.

"I cannot wear my giraffe pants to the mall," I say in my best grown-up voice.

Brianna nods like she understands, but then she says, "You could wear your karate outfit. That would be sorta fancy and plain." Brianna starts giggling because she knows she's being silly.

It's very hard to explain something to a four-year-old.

"Brianna!" I shout, tired of being patient. "Can't you just do me this solid?" I ask this too loud and I'm pretty sure she's going to start crying, and if that happens, I'll be in trouble, but instead she puts her hands on her hips and stares up at me.

"What do I get?" she asks.

"You're not supposed to get anything for doing a solid. That's the point." But since I really want her to do it, I add, "I will watch *Mammoth Lake* 5 with you when I get back."

A big smile lights up her face. I don't actually mind watching a kiddie movie but it's important I pretend that I do so Brianna thinks it's a favor. There are like fifteen Mammoth Lake movies. They are animated and have brightly colored sea creatures that always get in trouble and Brianna and I have watched number five (her favorite) about one hundred times.

"Okay," she says.

We shake hands. "Solid," I say, and nod, all serious.

"Solid," she says.

Twenty minutes later when Brianna runs in my room, screaming, "Plain clothes, plain clothes!" I scream too.

I mean *really*. I'm in my underwear! I have two outfits on my bed, and I was just waiting to see which one I was going to put on. I sure wasn't waiting for a pint-size screaming missile to fly into my room. I can hear Naomi talking to Momma downstairs, and I hiss at Brianna, "You were supposed to tell me before she came to the door."

"I didn't know she was here until she rang the bell."

I don't know why I thought Brianna would've just sat at the kitchen window staring out at the street until Naomi showed up. I push Brianna out of my room and quickly pull on my clothes and head downstairs. At least Brianna had gotten Naomi's outfit right. She is definitely "plain clothes!" in her crop pants and tank.

Naomi and I walk side by side to her mom's car, comparing our toenail polish and discussing whether we should have cinnamon pieces or a hot pretzel once we get to Shoreline. Nikila is already in the car and Mara is meeting us there after her volleyball practice.

Momma walks right behind us, and she bends into the window to talk to Naomi's mom, Audrey.

Audrey won't let us call her Mrs. De La Cruz and will only answer us if we call her by her first name. Naomi says her mom thinks it sounds old to be called Mrs. Somebody. I think it's cool to call someone's mom by their first name, but Momma doesn't like it. Whenever I have to tell my mother something Audrey said, I always call her Mrs. De La Cruz.

I give Momma one minute to get all the logistics figured out. (Logistics is when moms compare notes and make sure everyone has the same plan for the day.) When a minute is up, I pull her arm. "We gotta go, Momma," I say.

"Have fun, girls," she says, but she sounds like she is really saying "Be careful."

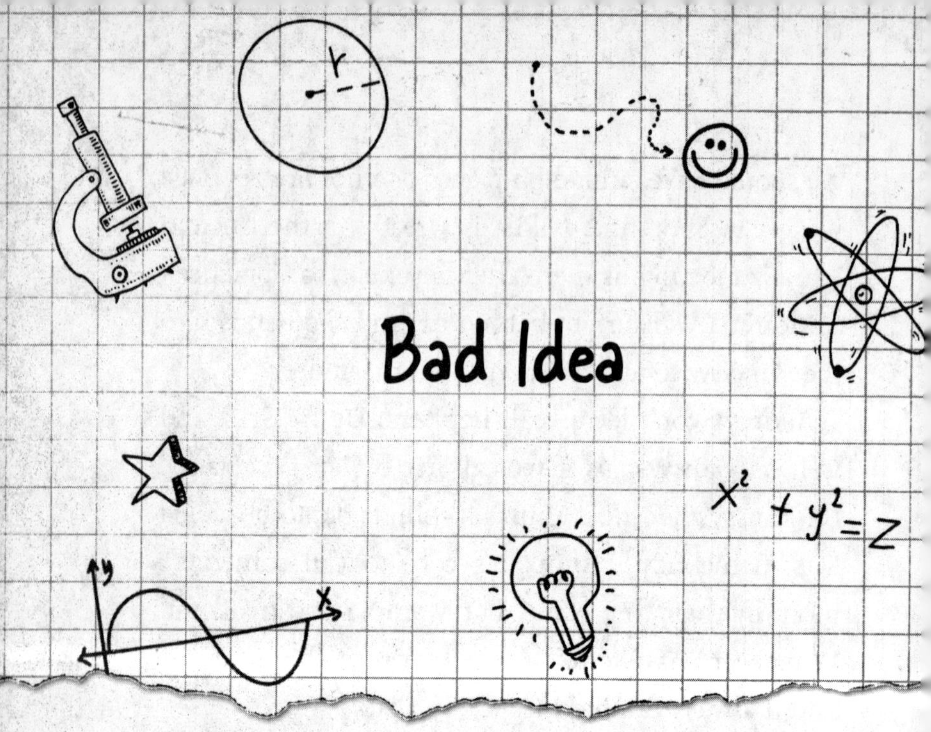

Bad Idea

When we get to Shoreline, we see right away it's deader than a bug on the windshield.

"Whose great idea was this?" Naomi complains.

We walk in and right back out of a small, cramped clothes store and peek inside a place selling fancy stuff for gardens and then wander all the way over to Trader Joe's.

"Let's get some coffee," Naomi suggests.

In the back of Trader Joe's, they have a sample area and on the counter, they have tiny paper cups sitting next to a silver jug of hot coffee. Whenever we shop here, Momma always gets a tiny free cup of coffee.

She let me taste it once. Gross.

I don't want to get any coffee, but I don't say that. I just follow behind Naomi and Nikila. If they are doing it. I am doing it too, but I notice Nikila is biting her thumbnail, so she probably doesn't think it's a great idea either.

We pass through the fresh produce section, which smells like strawberries but is way too cold, and head to the back of the store. At the sample station, we line up behind an old man who is taking a long, long time to make his cup of coffee. I wonder if I should ask him if he needs any help, since he is sort of trembly and has a cane hooked on his arm. I'm not sure if he is going to be able to make the coffee and hold it without spilling it all over his shirt and the floor. It reminds me of Brianna when she was younger and refused to let anybody help her do stuff and she'd try to pour herself juice and make a huge mess.

"An alien has infected the elder population on Earth," Naomi says. "They have taken over their bodies, but they are trying to fight them. You can tell who is infected because they shake so much!"

"Naomi!" I hiss. "Shhhhh."

Naomi just laughs and nudges Nikila who laughs along and then Naomi does a fake overly dramatic sigh and a big eye roll, as if she has been waiting *forever* for her turn to get coffee. I pause and then sigh and eye roll even though it seems mean. It's not like he can help being old, but I am trying to be grown-up, which means getting impatient. Finally, he gets his coffee fixed and with one shaky hand holding his small cup, and the other shaky hand trying to manage his cane, he struggles away from the counter. I watch him go, hoping he makes it to some safe bench somewhere.

"Alien!" Naomi whispers loudly and cackles.

As Nikila makes herself a cup of coffee, the woman behind the counter, who is fixing up samples of pita bread slices with glops of reddish hummus, starts watching us, and that makes me nervous.

Are we supposed to be doing this?

Naomi makes her cup, but before I can make mine, the woman making samples faces us, holding her knife full of hummus over another slice of pita.

"Are you girls here with somebody?" she asks.

"Yes, ma'am," Naomi lies. "My mom is in the frozen section. She told us to get some coffee, 'cause it's so cold over there."

I have long been in awe of Naomi's ability to make up things that sound absolutely true, right on the spot.

I put three pumps of coffee in my little cup, pour

in some cream, and because I'm trying to be super speedy, I skip adding sugar. I smile apologetically at the woman. "Thanks," I say, as if she gave me something.

"Sure thing," she says. "Now you girls scoot."

We scoot right out the store. When we get back into the hot outside, we burst out laughing.

Naomi says in a loud voice, "That lady was ridic! Like she's the boss of the coffee."

Naomi thinks a lot of things are "ridic." I don't think the woman is ridiculous. She usually seems nice. She always lets me take an extra sample when I'm grocery shopping with Momma.

Nikila giggles, like she agrees with Naomi.

And I feel my head bob up and down like I think so too.

"Let's go to Winchey's," Naomi says, tossing her still-full cup into the trash. So the whole idea to get coffee seems ridic if you ask me.

"That'd be fun!" Nikila says.

Winchey's is an arcade on Bay Street. It *would* be fun, but going there was not part of the plan. I'd need to ask Momma if it would be okay to leave Shoreline. And I know exactly what she would say: no way. Momma is not a fan of plans changing. She might even say she should just pick me up.

"Winchey's is great, but . . ." I start. I don't know what to say that will make my friends see leaving Shoreline is a bad idea, without making me sound like an immature rule follower. "Uh, isn't Mara meeting us in like an hour?" I try.

"We could send her a text," Naomi says. She pulls a lip gloss egg from her pocket and smears it on.

"Yeah, but . . ." I pause and Naomi stares at me, holding her gloss in her hand like she might throw it at me if I say the wrong thing. "Her mom would have to drop her off at Winchey's," I explain. "And wouldn't that be weird since your mom dropped us off here?"

Naomi shrugs, as if what I said didn't matter at all, but I can see Nikila is worried. I wish she would say it is a bad idea. I don't want to be the one to have to say it.

"But if everybody wants to go . . ." I say, forcing the words out past a bubble of air stuck in my throat.

I'm so relieved when Nikila says, "We should wait for Mara."

I don't know what I'll do when Mara gets here.

Maybe my experiment isn't such a great idea after all.

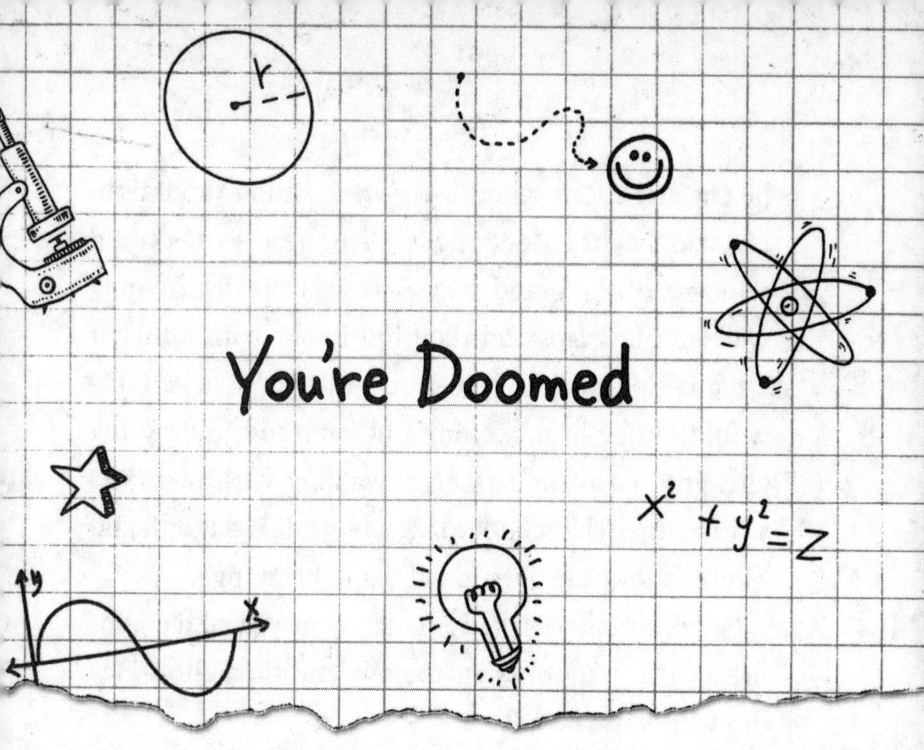

You're Doomed

But when Mara comes, Naomi doesn't want to leave Shoreline anymore because by then, Cory Aquino has shown up. He is with his cousin Wesley who is one year older than us.

Naomi has a crush on Cory. She pretends this isn't true. When we ask her about liking Cory she says we are being ridic, but then she'll get a little goofy grin. And say things like how she likes when boys have their hair cut in a fade (which is how Cory's hair is cut) and how she likes when boys wear colorful Vans (which is what Cory wears).

Momma doesn't like Cory. Ever since she found out

he cheated at our school's big walk-a-thon fundraiser. He said he had done eighty laps, just so he could win one of the grand prize bikes. But really, he only walked a few laps and then hid in the bathroom for a big chunk of the walk. I guess he thought nobody would notice him slinking out later and joining the lead group as if he had been walking with them the whole time. The school made a huge deal out of it and Momma said she questioned his upbringing.

Cory's parents donated a bunch of playground equipment to the school as an apology and then all us kids thought he was cool.

"So tell us all the teachers to avoid at Douglas," Naomi asks Wesley. Wesley started at Douglas last year, so he can give us the scoop on all the seventh-grade stuff.

I've noticed that Naomi has been talking to Wesley instead of Cory and I am guessing it is to prove she doesn't like Cory. This seems silly to me but for all I know maybe it is the grown-up way to do things.

"You're doomed if you get Mrs. Winters!" Wesley crows, sounding like he is hoping at least one of us will get her.

"Is she really hard?" Nikila asks, sounding worried.

Nikila worries about school stuff more than the rest

of us. I think it's because one of her aunties gives her fifty dollars for every good report card. But we don't even have our classes yet, so there is no reason for her to think she is going to have to suffer through this Winters person, but it's clear she's already freaked out.

Nikila's frown deepens when Wesley says, "She's the hardest English teacher at Douglas. She's the hardest *teacher* at Douglas. If you get her, drop her, or your first year is gonna be totally messed up."

We all nod our agreement for dropping Winters, but I don't really know what dropping a teacher means, and besides, I'm sure I can handle a hard English teacher. I don't worry about grades like Nikila does, but I like school. I like learning things. Naomi calls me a smarty-pants sometimes and tries to make it seem like I should be embarrassed for being in GATE (that's the gifted program). But I like GATE. Even though my friends aren't in it with me, for an hour once a week I get to work on tricky logic problems and learn tough vocabulary words.

We sit down at some metal tables outside Bagel Street Café, even though the tables are only for customers. There's a guy sitting at a table smoking a cigarette and he sort of nods at us. A sign on the wall says No Smoking but he obviously doesn't care. His hair is all matted and he has about a thousand friendship bracelets on. I nudge Mara.

"He must have a lot of friends," I say. I'm just clowning around but Mara laughs super hard and repeats what I said loud enough for the man to hear.

He looks at us and then looks at his bracelets and starts fumbling around with them and I wish I hadn't said anything. I get the fuzzy caterpillar in my nose feeling. If the man is mad and starts yelling at us, I know I'll cry.

"Are you guys coming to my party?" Cory asks us and the caterpillar crawls away and my eyes get wide with excitement.

I did not come up with my experiment idea because of Cory's party. I wasn't even thinking about Cory's party, but still this is the type of thing I *could've* been thinking about.

When Cory handed me the invitation last week, I had smiled at him and said "Sounds like a blast, Cory," but inside I was thinking, *Momma is not going to let me go.*

I had known with the way Momma thinks about Cory and his "upbringing" she would have thought me going to a party at his house would be a bad idea, so I hadn't even asked her about it yet. Now though, she'd have to let me go. Assuming my friends *are* going.

I look at them eagerly.

Mara nods. "*Everybody's* going, right?" she asks.

"Yeah," Naomi says.

My stomach feels like it is full of warm hot cocoa and my smile feels big enough to put holes in my cheeks. "If everybody's going," I say, "then I'm dutely, tutely going." I'm so brilliant for coming up with my experiment.

"I don't know if I can go," Nikila says, sort of quiet, and she starts picking at her nails.

"You have to go, Nik!" I almost shout.

"Well, my mom and dad don't really like boy-girl parties."

"But that's ridiculous," Mara says, then quickly adds, "Sorry, Nik."

Nikila just shrugs like she has no problem with Mara thinking her parents are ridiculous.

"But it's a *promotion* party. For the *whole* sixth grade," Naomi says, as if she needs to convince Nikila.

"I'll ask them," Nikila says, but she doesn't sound confident.

The man with the bracelets stubs out his cigarette and walks over to our table and I am sure he's going to say something mean or ask us for money. Now that he's closer I can smell the heat of too many days outside rolling off him and see how dirty his hands are. He rips off one of his bracelets and hands it out to me.

Now, everyone knows you're not supposed to rip friendship bracelets off—it's bad luck. "No, thank you," I say, and my face feels like it's stuck in a deep fryer. My friends start giggling but it's not a bit funny.

"You take it," the man says, his voice is gruff and crackly. "I got enough."

"Take it! Take it!" Cory and Wesley both start shouting and the fuzzy caterpillar is back. It's tickling my nose and any second my eyes could start watering. I can't see how to not take the bracelet since the man is standing there not moving, holding it out to me. It's an orange and yellow one, and I love those colors, but it must've been on the man for a long time because the colors are faded, and the bracelet is filthy. I don't want it. I don't want to touch it.

My bottom lip starts to tremble.

"Don't make her cry," Naomi says.

She doesn't say it meanly. But that doesn't matter. I am breathing through my mouth so I don't have to smell anything but when I look into the man's eyes, they are shining at me. The tears that were threatening to sneak up my throat and out of my eyes go right back down and I hold out my hand for the bracelet.

He drops it in my hand like he knows I would rather he didn't touch me and then he nods and shuffles away.

"Gross," Mara says. "Throw that away!"

I don't like how loud she says it, but I know she's right. Still, I tuck the bracelet in my pocket. Maybe if I wash it, it won't be so gross.

Then the boys get up and start messing around, calling each other names and stuff and trying to step on each other's shoes. Wesley jumps up on the little wall of the fountain even though I know you're not supposed to do that. Cory pretends like he's going to push Wesley into the water.

One of the workers from Bagel Street comes outside and we all run before we get yelled at. It's kind of scary and kind of fun. Like a roller coaster.

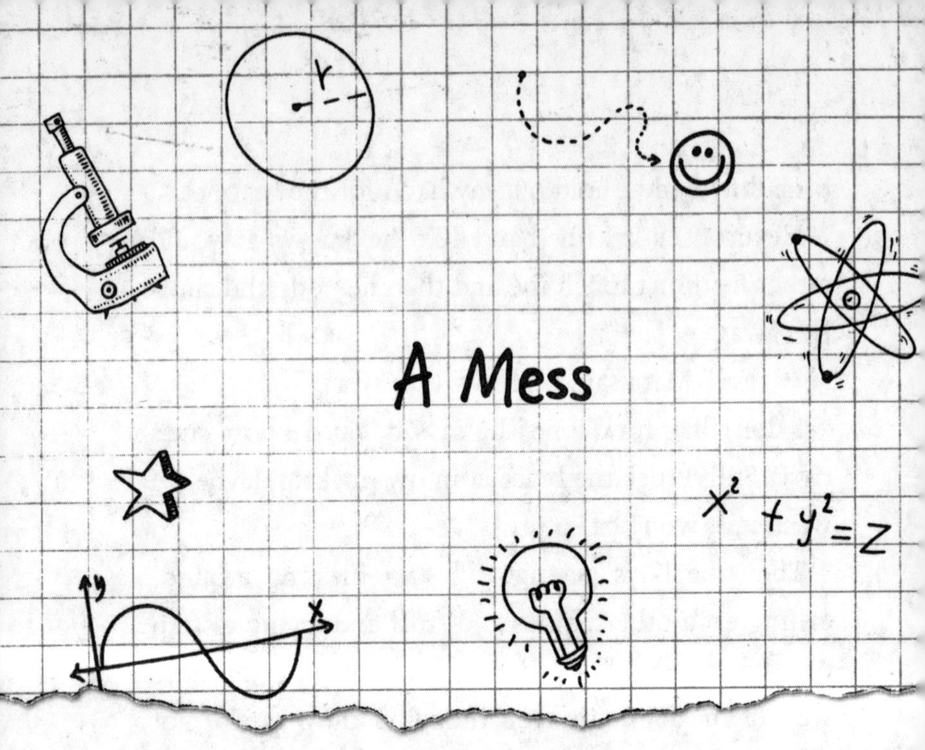

A Mess

Hanging out with Cory and Wesley isn't at all like hanging out with just my friends. Cory and Wesley are loud, even when clerks are staring at them, and they bump into each other and race around. They are like puppies.

When Nikila, Naomi, Mara, and I all squeal over how cute the stuffed animal pyramid is in the Toy Safari window, the boys don't even stop to look.

And they aren't even embarrassed when we go inside CVS, and they crash into a display making sunglasses fall all over the floor. They just run away laughing.

Mara shouts at them to come back, but they ignore

her and even though we didn't make the mess, Nikila, Mara, and I pick up the glasses. Naomi helps for a second, but then she says she better check on the boys to make sure they aren't causing any more trouble. I'm sure she just wants to spend a little more time with Cory. And when Mara, Nikila, and I leave CVS, I'm clearly right, because Naomi is already outside with the boys.

"You think you're sly but I'm on to you," I tell her and her eyebrows squeeze together and her cheeks get red. I didn't mean to embarrass her and I quickly say, "I'm just kidding!"

Her face relaxes and I'm glad that we're not going to argue.

"Let's go to Winchey's," Wesley says. "This place is for losers."

My stomach does a little uncomfortable rumble, but Mara shakes her head.

"I don't have Winchey's money," she says. "Besides, we're gonna be picked up soon."

I'm impressed at how easy it is for Mara to say real things without worrying how someone might take it or if they will think you are a baby or a weirdo. Maybe that is being mature.

"Whatever," Wesley says.

"Later," Cory says and then they both run off howling and laughing.

Naomi seems disappointed that the guys left, but I'm relieved that it's just me and my friends again. I didn't realize until Cory and Wesley were gone how uncomfortable I had been when they were around.

There are some katas in karate that are very intense, and you have to hold yourself really tight and think about every move. I always feel exhausted after doing those types of katas and I feel the same way now. It's almost like I had to pretend to be someone else instead of being the real Kylie. The thought gives me a little pinch. Is my whole experiment about not really being me? I quickly dismiss the thought though because I am certain that the real me is not an immature crybaby. The whole point of my experiment is to prove that. And to prove that me and my friends should be just as close in seventh grade as we have been all through elementary school.

Naomi's mom picks us up a little while later, and as soon as she gets in the car, Naomi says, "Mom, you have to convince Mr. and Mrs. Kumar to let Nikila go to Cory's party."

Nikila ducks her head down and starts nibbling on her nails.

"But of course, you have to go, Nikila!" Audrey says. "It's for your whole class."

I can't help smiling because Naomi and her mom sound exactly alike. I'm also smiling because I know with Audrey on the case, Nikila will get to go to the party, which means everybody is going, which means, I get to go.

Naomi puts on a pair of black sunglasses that have rhinestones on the edges.

"Ooh," I say. "Where'd you get those?"

Naomi turns around and faces me. I can't see her eyes behind the glasses. "From CVS," she says, like I should know that.

Audrey glances over at the glasses. "I hope they weren't expensive, Nooms. You know I need you to be more careful about spending money."

"They were on sale, Mom," Naomi says, sounding very bored with this whole conversation.

"Sale doesn't mean cheap," Audrey says. "I told you there's going to be some—"

Naomi cuts her mom off.

"I know!" she says.

I look at Audrey, but she is just looking at the road ahead. Momma wouldn't like it at all if I used that tone with her. She'd say, *Don't use that tone with me, Kylie.*

The car is quiet while Naomi sits all sulky faced, and Nikila, Mara, and I pretend we don't notice.

Naomi slides the sunglasses on top of her head.

She must've bought them while we were cleaning up the boys' mess. I wish she had told me she was getting them. I would've bought a pair too. I want to ask Naomi why she didn't tell us she was buying sunglasses, but she is wearing a don't-talk-to-me face. I'm a good enough friend to leave her alone.

Mara says, "I wish I could wear cute sunglasses." She takes her regular glasses off and glares at them. Then she stretches her arms out and pats my cheeks. "Nik? Is that you?" she jokes. Even Naomi laughs and Mara puts her glasses back on.

When I get home, I ask Momma if I can change my hypothesis. "It could be that I think I will be more mature when I do what everybody is doing, when it's something I want to do. Like you know making, um, informed choices." I hadn't liked nodding along when Naomi talked badly about the lady giving samples, or how I drank a little cup of coffee even though I didn't like the taste.

Momma gives me one of those looks that means she is very amused by me and for a tiny second I think she is going to say my idea is great but then she says, "So what you're saying is, you want to test if you'll be happier if you get to do just what you want to do?" That's not exactly what I said, but it doesn't matter because I can tell by the way she asks the question she did not think my idea was great and that I am being a very poor scientist. She doesn't even bother waiting for me to answer, she just walks away laughing and shaking her head, which means, no way do I get to change my hypothesis.

OBSERVATIONS

> Drinking coffee is gross. Even if everybody else is drinking coffee, it is still gross. I don't know why it's a grown-up thing to drink it.
> Some people think being mean is funny but making fun of nice people does not feel good.
> Boys care less about what people think about them than girls. (Maybe this is not true of all boys.) Is caring about what people think more or less grown-up?
> Even people who are unhoused could have friends.
> Sometimes people act really weird about liking someone. It seems like it would be more mature to just be honest about it.
> I can wear cute sunglasses and I wish I had a pair like Naomi's.

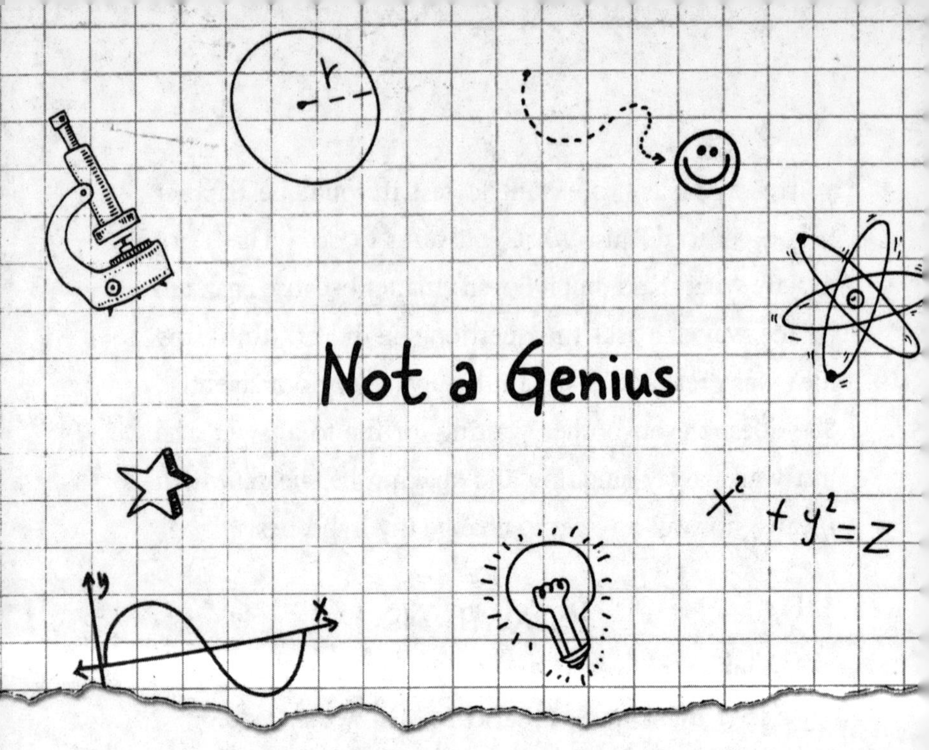

Not a Genius

Dad finally gets home from his business trip, and after we have chowed through the chili dogs we picked up from Sloppy House, we look through the pictures Momma had printed out from my promotion. She said she wants to put them in a scrapbook, but I'm pretty sure they will just sit in the box with the other pictures she plans to scrapbook.

Momma already texted all the pictures she took that day to him, but he stares at them like they are completely new.

"Wow, what a knockout," he says as he looks at a picture of me standing in front of the flagpole.

I want to put the pictures away.

"You have your mother's eyes," he says and then gives a long whistle. "Watch out, now!"

"Watch out for what, Daddy?" Brianna asks, but before he can answer her, she demands, "What about my eyes, Daddy? Are my eyes like Momma's too?"

He gives her a hug and a raspberry kiss on her neck. "You have Uncle Ollie's eyes, I'm afraid," he teases.

Uncle Ollie is my dad's uncle, and he is very old and has buggy eyes with saggy, droopy lids.

"Daddy!" Brianna squeals, knowing he's only pulling her leg.

If he's only teasing about Brianna's eyes, does that mean he isn't serious about mine? I look at Momma and I look at my picture. Maybe I have her eyes. "I wish I had known not to wear a dress," I say.

"What do you mean, 'known'?" he asks, making little quotation marks in the air.

I sigh heavily. It can be difficult explaining things to my dad. "Everybody was *casual*, Dad. Didn't you see that?"

"I only had eyes for you," he says looking at one of the pictures, and then he looks back at me. "But I'll tell you something." He holds up a finger. "On this trip, I saw a *lot* of stylish folks. And you could tell the women who were sure of themselves. They held their heads up, they walked with purpose, they dressed with flair." He raises another finger for each point.

"Were they all wearing dresses?" I ask, thinking if that's what he meant, why didn't he just say so?

"No. Some were, but some were in pants, or suits."

"So, I should've worn a suit for promotion?"

Dad throws his head back and laughs like I'm the funniest girl.

"What's so funny?" Brianna asks.

Yeah, what? I wonder.

"No, Ky, I wasn't saying you should've worn a suit."

"What *are* you saying?" Momma asks. She sounds a little exasperated, but I know she's not really mad. This is how a lot of conversations go with my dad. Maybe it's because Momma, Brianna, and I spend so much time together without him around. Or maybe it's that we're all girls and he's a guy. But sometimes it's like the three of us speak one language and he speaks a different one, so we don't know what he's talking about.

"I'm saying," he starts talking really slow, like that will make it easier to understand him, "it didn't matter what they wore, it was how they carried themselves. If you are confident and carry yourself that way, then you can wear anything. And if you are the incredibly amazing Kylie Stanton, you can easily handle being the only girl to wear a dress. It shows you got style."

"I wasn't the only one," I admit.

"What?" he asks, leaning back into the couch cushions and letting his mouth fall open. "What other fabulous lady dared to step apart from the crowd?"

Very softly I say, "Melody Zacharias."

"She must be a genius," he says.

I see Momma give the smallest shake of her head at him. Even Momma knows Melody is not the girl you want to be grouped with.

"Not a genius?" Dad asks.

I shrug. For all I know, Melody could be a genius. In fact, she probably is. That could be why she's such a weirdo.

"A woman of great taste?" he asks.

I shake my head hard. But as soon as I do, I realize I don't really know anything about Melody except she eats her lunch alone outside the school office and back in first grade she peed her pants in class.

"Rob, stop being such a nut," Momma says.

"I see what happened here," Dad says like he has just discovered electricity. "She's a spy! She knew exactly who to watch to see how to be one of the best-dressed girls at graduation—"

"Promotion," I interrupt. It's a waste of time to

correct him, because he already knows.

"Whateverrrrr," he says.

"Dad!"

He leans forward and puts his hands on his knees and stares at me. "She found out what you were wearing, and had her mom buy that too." His voice gets really low. "And you never suspected a thing."

I would find the whole thing a lot funnier if it wasn't for my experiment. Not like I'm going around spying on my friends or anything, but I *am* trying to copy them.

I see Momma is looking at me. She rolls her eyes and I roll mine back. It's our little way of saying Dad is just too ridiculous. But as silly as he is, we're all so glad that he's home.

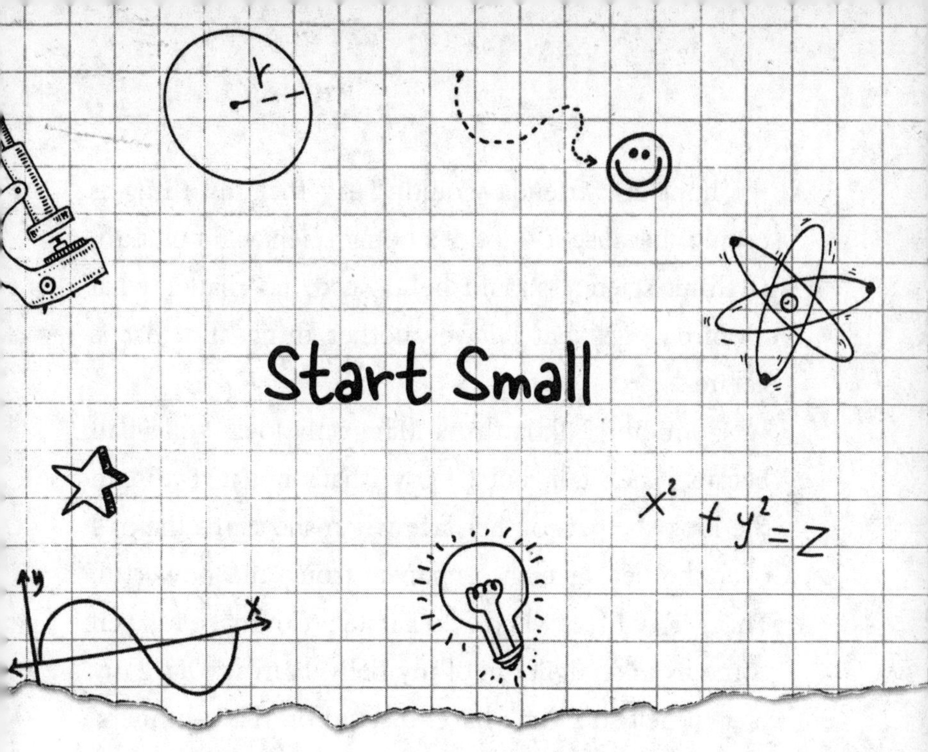

Start Small

My friends and I don't do every single thing together. We all have our own things too. Like Naomi loves pretending and wants to go to drama camp this summer. She asked me if I wanted to go too and I said "No *thanks!*" I would not want to get on a stage and perform in front of people.

Nikila loves music and says she's going to start a rock band when she's older, but I'm not sure if there are that many rock bands with piano players (that's the instrument she plays). But maybe she will be the next Alicia Keys. Mara's thing is sports, but volleyball especially.

I hope my friends wouldn't say that my thing is crying, because it's not. It's being sciency about stuff. (I think sciency should be a word, no matter what Momma says) but I have another thing and that is karate.

Naomi and Nikila think Mara only loves volleyball because she's tall, but I know that's not it. I've seen the look she gets on her face when she slams the ball over the net. Like she is super strong and powerful. That's how I feel when I do karate. I can make my yell come from straight out of my belly. I already have my brown belt so I don't have to stand on the beginners' side of the dojo anymore.

I like to get to the dojo early so I can practice before class. Usually Momma brings her computer and a bunch of files and acts like the corner of the dojo is her office. I wish she would watch me so she could see how good my moves are getting. Today she and Dad just dropped me and Brianna off and they went somewhere together.

I'm practicing a kata called the Praying Mantis on the advanced side of the dojo, when I see Mr. Kim coming my way. I hope he wants to tell me how impressed he is with me.

What he says instead is, "You have been working hard,

Kylie. When are you going to test for your advanced brown belt?"

This isn't the first time he's asked me this. At our winter tournament, when I won a first-place trophy with my bo staff routine, he asked me the same thing. Testing for the next level belt is hard, but I haven't minded it before now. Even though I get nervous standing in front of all the sensei, it's been my chance to show how well I've learned all the different katas and forms and weapons routines. But to move up a belt now, not only would I have to do all the regular stuff for the test, I'd also have to demonstrate a routine I created myself. From scratch.

I have no idea how to come up with my own routine. I asked Mr. Kim if he could just teach me a harder one and I could do that for my test, but he explained the whole point was creating one. But I know if I make up a routine it will be bad. It won't get me my advanced brown belt. It might even get me laughed at. And that would probably make me cry. I just want Mr. Kim to show me stuff and I'll learn it. I will probably be a brown belt forever.

"Um," I say, trying hard to think of a way to answer Mr. Kim. All that comes to me is the truth. "I haven't come up with a routine yet."

"Still?" he asks, sounding shocked, and as if he doesn't know me at all. "What are you waiting for?"

"I wish you'd just teach me something." I mumble, because I know he won't like it.

"Kylie, you can do this. Just trust yourself a little." Mr. Kim is tall with muscely arms, and he has dark, dark brown eyes that have a way of piercing all the way to my mushy middle. His hair is gray, and he has wrinkles around his mouth and eyes but when we went to Las Vegas for a tournament last year, he was the one doing flips in the pool and playing shark attack like a kid. His daughter came to Vegas too and every time Mr. Kim introduced her to an instructor from another dojo his chest would puff up and you could tell he thought she was the greatest thing in the world. I wonder if Dad talks about me when he is on his business trips or if he forgets all about me.

Mr. Kim nudges me toward the big mirrors in the front of the class. "Go and practice. Do only a couple of movements. Things you know but in a new way. Start small. Let your mind relax and you'll be surprised with what you can come up with."

I stand in front of the mirrors, trying to make my mind relax and allow an awesome routine to get planted there but nothing comes to me.

There are a couple of black belts practicing in the back of the dojo. I turn and watch them to see if I could maybe copy them.

But then I see Mr. Kim watching me watch the black belts, and I have a bad feeling he knows I wasn't letting my mind relax. Copying isn't something you want to get caught doing.

After my class is over (and I still haven't come up with a single move for my routine, except to bow at the beginning, which you have to do anyway) I sit and watch the little kids' class.

Brianna is a yellow belt, which is one up from the white beginning belt. Watching Brianna do karate is almost the only time when she is very serious. She bows at her sensei, Miss Senta, and then Brianna gets low in her karate stance.

In the middle of her class, when kids are practicing different things, I see Brianna walk up to Miss Senta and ask if she can show her something. Most of the sensei at our dojo really like Brianna because even though she's so little, she works hard.

I'm amazed when I see her show Miss Senta a kata . . . that Brianna created herself! Okay, it's not the best kata in the world. There are a bunch of turns and kicks that look pretty random, but it is clearly

Brianna's own creation.

How did she do that? My mouth hangs open a little, and my hands clench together. I hope her routine ends soon. When it does, Miss Senta gives her a little pat on the head. If I come up with a great routine, Mr. Kim will not pat me on the head. He will bow and I'll bow back. And that will be better.

After karate, when Momma and Dad pick us up, they are holding hands and that makes me smile. It's nice seeing them like this.

On the drive home, Brianna tells them how much Miss Senta liked her kata.

"Of course, she did," Dad says. Momma glances at me in the rearview mirror.

"How did you think of the moves?" I ask Brianna.

Brianna gives me a puzzled look. "I just put all the stuff I like together," she explains, making it sound like it is the most obvious thing ever.

"But . . ." I am not sure what I want to say. I look out the window at the cars going past. Jazz is playing on the radio, and it is that kind that goes in all different directions. It is sort of jumbled and it matches how I feel. I am used to teaching Brianna things, not the other way around. "Weren't you a little nervous to show Miss Senta? What if she didn't like it?"

"Kylie," Momma warns. She doesn't like when I

share stuff I worry about with Brianna. *We don't need you filling her brain up with big girl problems yet*, Momma has told me a bunch of times.

But Brianna just says, "So what? I like it." Then she bumps her head into my arm and starts purring like she's a kitty.

"That's it, Bree Bree," Dad says, sounding more proud of her than I think he should be. Aren't we *supposed* to care what our teachers think?

Later, I stand in my room, gripping the carpet with my toes and I try to let my brain take over, and show me some awesome routine, but my brain doesn't seem to be speaking to me at the moment.

Maybe I should've told Mr. Kim coming up with my own moves completely goes against my experiment. Somehow, I don't think he'd understand.

I wonder if Brianna would create a routine for me.

I try just twirling around, and after a minute, I don't have any great ideas, but I'm super dizzy.

There's a tap on my door and then Dad comes in my room.

"Hey, you," he says. "Momma said you're working on a new kata? Going to test for your advanced brown soon?"

I wish I could say yes, but all I do is shrug.

"Ky, if you don't believe in yourself, nobody else is going to. You know that, right?"

"I guess," I say.

"Momma also told me about some experiment? Going along with the crowd?"

I can tell by his tone that he doesn't think much of the idea. "That's not exactly what it is," I say. "It's testing group thinking and it's going to prove how mature I am." He still looks doubtful, so I add, "I totally believe that I am mature. And I thought of the experiment all by myself."

Dad laughs at that. "I guess you got me there." Then he bows to me like we're in the dojo and then he does some ridiculous moves that are even sillier than Brianna's. "You can have those for free," he says. "Don't stay up too late." He gives me a kiss good night and leaves the room.

Once he's gone, I stare in the mirror. The girl staring back at me smiles. Then we bow to each other.

I bounce up and down on the soft carpet to get pumped up, then I do a couple of kicks and twirls. Nothing that feels like a real beginning of my own kata, but at least I don't feel so hopeless. Maybe I *can* do it.

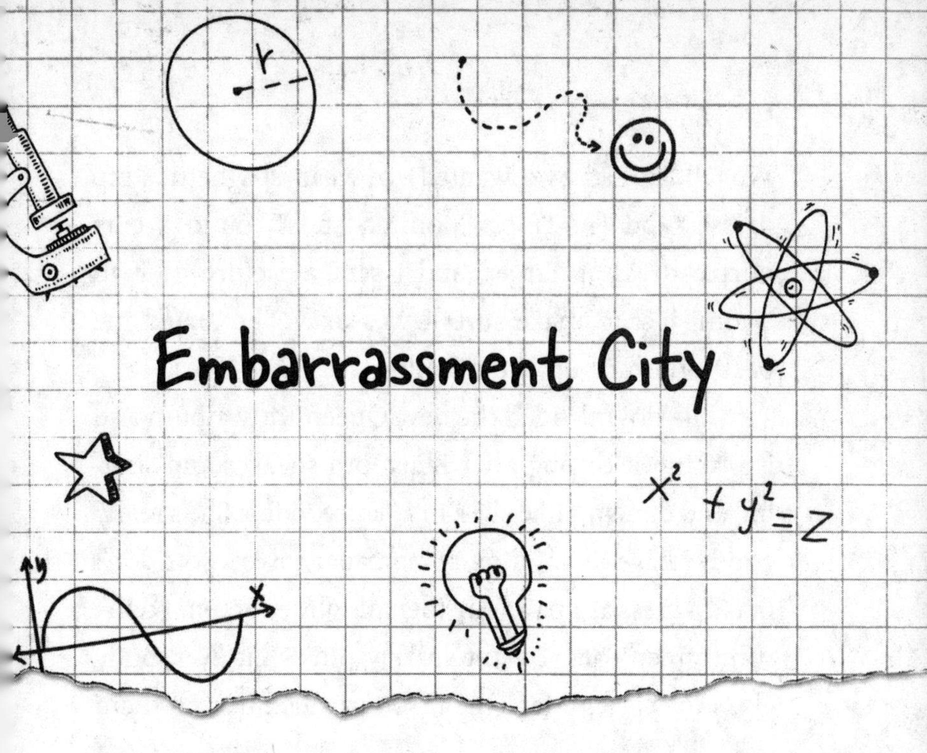

Embarrassment City

I was right about Audrey working her magic on Mr. and Mrs. Kumar, because one week later, we are all at Naomi's getting ready for Cory's party. Dad had to leave on another trip, but this one is just for a couple of days. It is the first time that I was glad he was gone because I knew Momma still wasn't that happy about me going to Cory's for a party and if Dad had been home, he probably would have made a big deal about me not doing stuff that Momma isn't 100 percent sure of. And no way did I want to miss the party.

Tonight, I'm not at all worried about what I'm wearing.

We all agreed we wanted to wear spaghetti strap dresses and flip-flops. Momma and I found a cute purple dress at Target, and I sent a picture of it to Naomi just to make sure it was okay. She texted me back a thumbs-up and a smiley face and a heart.

Nikila downloaded the new Queen Kitty album and is playing it through her Bluetooth speaker and singing and dancing like she's in a dance video. She's really good. I have my feet on some paper towels so I don't make a mess as I paint my toenails glitter green. I don't want green toes. I want sparkly pink. But everybody else's toes are glitter green, so I'm stuck having them too.

When we get to Cory's, I find out it is super, super cool to have a father who fixes vending machines and arcade games for a living. In their family room, there's a pinball machine, a table where two people can sit down and play *Super Mario Bros.*, and even one of those games where you can pretend to drive a race car. How awesome is that? Although I'm sure I would miss my parents and Brianna, I wouldn't mind if Cory's family adopted me for a few weeks. I would love to be able to play pinball every day . . . for *free*.

There is music playing and Cory's parents must think kids will start dancing, because the furniture is all pressed against the walls, making an empty space in the middle of the room. I love to dance, and I hope it's not like when Ms. Rosenthal had a class party for us in fourth grade and put on music, but everybody was too embarrassed to even sway.

Melissa Nelson and Miriam Park start doing some wild moves in the middle of the floor. They are best friends. They like to be called M&M, as if they are a piece of candy. And I haven't decided if that is cute or annoying.

Nobody else is dancing and I'm not about to join M&M. Besides, I really want a crack at the pinball machine. But there's already a line for it, so I'll have to wait for my chance to play.

Cory's mom sets out a ton of little bags of chips and candy bars and soda cans—I guess they get a deal on the stuff in vending machines. Before she disappears back into the kitchen she calls out, "We have a trampoline and Ping-Pong in the backyard if anyone's interested."

I'm very interested. Luckily, so are my friends.

My dad loves to garden but because he travels so much, he doesn't spend much time in the yard anymore and we probably have more weeds than pretty plants. I don't see a single weed in Cory's yard. The grass is dark green and there are large bushes all along the wooden fence with bright pink and white flowers. A big lemon tree is heavy with lemons as big as grapefruits, and I know Dad would be jealous of the line of roses that are by the sliding glass door. I take a big whiff of the flower-soaked air before following my friends to the trampoline.

"Isn't this great?" Naomi asks as she climbs through an opening in the safety netting.

"Dutely, tutely!" Nikila yells and Mara and I high-five each other.

A bunch of kids crowd onto the trampoline until there's hardly any room to jump. We're all yelling as we bounce, and it feels like we could jump up to the sky. The springs are stretching really far and the whole stand of the trampoline is shifting around but no one seems to care. With all the laughing and shouting, I can hardly catch my breath, so I climb through the slit in the net and escape to the lawn. Even though my friends are still jumping, I don't think I'm cheating on my experiment, because I did jump with them. I'm just taking a break.

I wander over to the Ping-Pong table that seems a little sad and lonely because no one is using it.

Then I hear a scream and turn around, expecting to

see a crashed trampoline, but instead it's just Lauren Kennedy flying across the yard, holding on to something that looks like handlebars. The handlebar thing is attached to a thick wire that goes from a tree on one side of the yard to another tree on the other side. Lauren screams again, but now that I can see her, I can tell it is one of those excited, I'm-having-so-much-fun screams and not oh-no-I'm-about-to-die screams. She reaches the other side and drops down to the ground.

"That was fantastic!" she yells. "Cory, you're so lucky!"

A bunch of kids scramble from the trampoline to get in line for their turn to fly across the yard, but I stand my ground by the Ping-Pong table.

"Come on!" Naomi shouts. "Everybody's gonna try the zip line!"

I wish she had phrased that differently.

I would prefer not to go flying across Cory's backyard on a zip line, screaming like I'm having so much fun. Not because I'm scared. I actually like going fast, and I have wanted to try zip-lining ever since we studied how gravity and air resistance and drag all combine to make zip lines work. I want to know how long it will take me to reach terminal velocity. Probably none of my friends that are shrieking across Cory's yard even care about the science like I do.

But I don't want to zip-line because, although my mother told me to put shorts underneath my dress so I could be more comfortable, I had told her I would be more comfortable without shorts. (The truth is, when I wear shorts under a dress, my bottom looks padded and square, and I'm not comfortable with that.) But I'm also not comfortable with a whole bunch of boys seeing my underwear. My dress lifted a little jumping on the trampoline, but my hands weren't raised above my head and there were too many people for my dress to really go *up*.

I'm not quite panicking but I know this is another math problem:

dress + zip line – shorts = embarrassment city

Somehow I have to make sure that *everyone* doesn't zip-line. If they all do it then I'm in big trouble. I amble over to my friends and join them in line.

"Nik," I whisper, pulling on her shoulder. "Are you wearing shorts?"

She looks down, like she can't quite remember, then shakes her head no. I wait for her to come to the same conclusion I did. It takes her about four seconds.

"Kylie and I are going to play Ping-Pong instead," she says to Mara, who is right in front of her. Then Nikila tugs at the hem of her dress. It's like a secret code or something, because Mara jumps out of line and the three of us head to the Ping-Pong table. I'm feeling so relieved until Naomi flashes us the shorts she is wearing under her dress. My eyebrows get close together and my lips get hard, but then I remember she isn't doing an experiment like I am.

The three of us play Ping-Pong like it is more fun than any silly zip line, but when Naomi's shrieks fill the backyard, we all turn to watch her.

"She should have told us to wear shorts," I say, the words coming out low and pitiful. I know I sound like a pouty baby, and worse, there is a tickle in my nose and my face feels too hot.

"Naomi doesn't need to tell us what to do," Mara says. Her glasses have slipped a little down her nose, and she gives them a nudge back up. "You could've worn shorts you know."

Mara's right but I am so disappointed that I still feel like I'm going to start bawling and no way can that happen. Not here!

Then Nikila pretends she's going to flash us her underwear. "Or you could you know just go for it!"

"Yeah, Kylie!" Mara says and acts like she is reaching for my dress. "Show us what you got!"

I run from her screaming and my tears get chased away.

A few minutes later when Naomi joins us and says we should ask Cory if we can come back over so we can all zip-line, I say, "Bet!"

Suddenly, the music coming from the house gets louder and everybody heads inside to see what's happening.

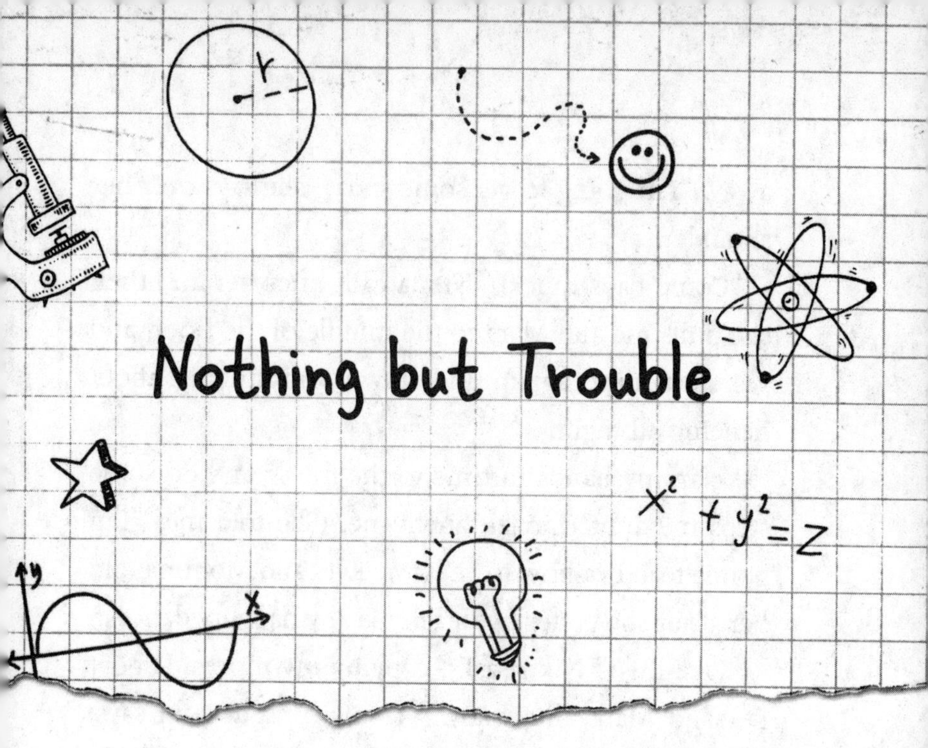

Nothing but Trouble

Cory's dad has turned the lights down a little so we can appreciate the spinning disco ball changing colors every few seconds. Julie Santos starts jumping in the middle of the floor like she's still on the trampoline. Pretty soon, a few girls join her, and then some boys and just like that, everybody's jumping around and shouting and dancing. Cory comes over and asks Naomi to dance with him and I am both shocked and impressed but she looks over at us and maybe it is because we are all grinning really hard at her, but she shakes her head hard no. He just shrugs and walks away and then asks Stacey Lee to dance.

Naomi's eyes narrow and then she starts to walk

away. "I'm going to get some soda," she says over her shoulder.

"Come back quick!" Nikila calls after her and then she pulls me and Mara to the middle of the floor, and we start jumping up and down and singing about dancing all night.

I clap my hands in time to the music and do some steps my aunt Harriet taught me. (She told me, "I'm gonna teach ya how to get *down*, Ky!" and Momma told her sister she better not teach me any naughty dances.)

"Like this?" Nikila asks, copying my moves. I show her and Mara all I know. Naomi runs up and says, "Show me too!" And if she was feeling bad about Cory dancing with Stacey, she isn't showing it now. The music gets faster and we're dancing hard and getting sweaty and banging into each other on purpose. When our favorite Queen Kitty song starts playing, we sing along so loud my throat starts to ache, but I don't stop.

Julie says everybody should meet at the beach next week and we all shout, "Yeah!"

I think Julie could've said we should all stand in traffic next week, and everyone would've said "Yeah!" because we're all having so much fun, we just want to keep going for the whole summer.

By the time the party is over, my face actually hurts from smiling so much, and I'm certain I have just had the best time of my entire life. My experiment is such an awesome idea. I cannot even imagine how low I would've felt if my friends had told me all about the party and I had been stuck at home, playing Zippy the Penguin with Brianna.

We are all spending the night at Naomi's, so when Audrey comes to pick us up, we go to their house. "Did y'all have fun?" Audrey asks, although we're all so giggly and sweaty, I'm sure it's obvious we did.

"Yes!" we all shout.

"Except for when Cory danced with someone else," Mara says, and gives Naomi's head a bop.

"Ow!" Naomi says. "And who cares about that?"

Audrey looks over at her and sighs. "Boys are nothing but trouble. Don't bother with them." She sounds a little annoyed, which is not the Audrey I am used to, but then she says, "Oh, shoot, don't listen to me. I still think of my sixth-grade crush. Robby. He was *so* cute." She pats her chest like her heart is beating too hard. "I wonder what he's doing now."

"Mom! Don't be gross," Naomi says and then we're all laughing again.

I send Momma a text letting her know I'm okay and having a great time and am safely back at Naomi's. She texts me back that she loves me and is glad I am having fun.

I wonder if she is lonely with just her and Brianna at home. Since I'm a lot older than my sister, I'm better company for Momma. Also, Momma isn't a big fan of Zippy the Penguin and can only play it for about twenty minutes before she starts getting fidgety and starts saying things like "How many times do we have to go around the igloo?" and "Are you sure you wouldn't rather watch TV?"

Whenever we stay over at Naomi's, we take over the basement. It isn't scary and dark like some basements, but a big room with large cushy sofas that are fun to bounce around on and an enormous television.

When we go downstairs to set up our sleeping bags, Mr. De La Cruz is already there. "You girls missed a great match," he tells us. "Toronto is going to be unbeatable this year!"

"Clear out, Daddy," Naomi says giving her dad a little nudge.

My chest gets tight and heavy. I wish my dad was around more so I could give him nudges and tell him to clear out when my friends are over.

Mr. De La Cruz says, "Let me just catch SportCenter," pretending like he's going to keep watching TV.

We all know he is just teasing, but Naomi says, "Dad!" in an angry voice, but then she smiles sweetly at him and says, "Go hang out with Mom; I bet she's lonely without you."

"I doubt that very much," Mr. De La Cruz says and his mouth turns down for a second. I don't think I've ever seen him look sad before. He usually is cracking a joke a minute. Almost like he heard my thoughts, his mouth turns back into its usual grin. He throws a pillow at Naomi and then gathers a few blankets from the sofa—I guess he must've got really comfy watching the game. "Okay, ladies, I can tell when I'm not wanted," he says, and after giving Naomi a funny salute, he heads upstairs.

"Men!" Naomi says all exasperated, and that makes us all start giggling. She sounds exactly like her mom.

"Can we watch something?" Mara asks.

"Dutely, *tutely*," Naomi says. "But we can't stream just *anything* because my mom will check to see."

"That's okay, 'cause look what I *brought*," Mara says and pulls a DVD out of her bag. There is a picture of a big blade with blood dripping off it, and a wide-open mouth that is obviously screaming. The mouth is wearing bright red lipstick and it is the same color as the blood on the knife. I put a hand over my own mouth, but that doesn't help, so I put both hands on my stomach. I hope I don't throw up.

A Big Crime

I don't like scary movies. Mara thinks scary movies are cool and is always telling us about some awful movie she saw with Mady.

Mara's brother is almost eighteen but even though he's older than us, he isn't very mature. At least it doesn't seem like it. Like when it comes to watching Mara, he has no clue he's not supposed to let her watch R-rated movies or drink triple-shot iced lattes or listen to songs full of bad words. I don't think her parents know he lets her do these things, but both of Mara's parents are nurses and they work long hours and so her brother is in charge of her a lot. Mara worries if he goes someplace far away for college, she will have to be home all by herself.

Staying by yourself sounds sort of exciting until you have to do it, and you realize houses make all sorts of weird noises that sound exactly like someone is sneaking in a downstairs window. I'm not a fan.

And I don't like the picture on Mara's DVD. "Ew," I say. "Gross." I am trying to launch a counterattack against the movie.

"What's it rated?" Naomi asks, almost like she can't breathe, and I don't know if that means she is excited or scared.

Mara turns the box over and after reading the back says, "R!" like she's found a dollar in her pocket.

"I can't watch that," Nikila says, and I'm so happy I want to hug her.

For a second Mara looks like she's going to argue, but then she just shrugs and puts the DVD back in her bag and pulls out another one.

My chest squeezes in.

"Okay, fine, this one is PG-13," she says like it is hugely painful to have to watch a PG-13 movie. Momma will sometimes let me watch those, as long as she knows exactly why it isn't just a straight up PG movie.

The picture on this one shows a girl who looks just a little older than us. Her hair is all ratty and matted and her face is dirty. Both her legs look broken, and she is looking like she sees something really horrible in the distance. I want Mara to put the box away. This does not look like a PG-13 my mom would let me watch.

I'm hoping Nikila will say she can't watch this movie either, but she just nods.

"Is it scary?" Naomi asks.

"It's *terrifying*," Mara says in a sinister voice.

Everyone laughs but me and then I remember my experiment and go, "huh, huh," which isn't exactly a laugh but is the closest I can come.

"We can't start screaming or anything," Naomi says as she slides the DVD into the player. "My mom or dad will have to check, and they'll make us turn the movie off."

I should be able to watch this movie. I'm sure a seventh grader is capable of watching a scary movie. And besides, all my friends are already squeezing together in front of the TV and giggling like they are waiting for the Giant Dipper roller coaster to start. I can't let them all ride away from me. I join them on the floor and offer a sad little giggle. How bad can it be? I ask myself.

Very, very bad. The movie has been on for only

fifteen minutes and I'm so scared, I can't move. I can't even swallow. I'm holding my knees really tight, and my nails are digging into my skin, but I can't stop. And I can't see anything because I'm keeping my eyes so tightly shut my cheeks hurt. But having my eyes shut doesn't help, because I can still hear. And hearing a scary movie is as bad as seeing one. It might even be worse. I know if I cover my ears, my friends will notice and think I'm a chicken. They won't want to be friends with a chicken.

Then Mara says, "Kylie, are your eyes shut?" like I'm committing some big crime.

I open my eyes and as soon as I do, I see the girl from the box cover standing next to an open grave. Before I can shut my eyes again, two hands pop out from the grave and grab her. I scream so loud it scares even me, and my friends say, "Shh, shh, shh!" but it is too late.

"Naomi?" Audrey calls as she starts coming down the stairs.

"Tell her you're fine," Naomi hisses at me and shuts the movie off.

When Audrey comes into the room, she snaps on the lights and looks at us without saying anything for a minute. I think she is waiting for one of us to start blabbing about what is going on, but no one says anything.

I'm trying to get my mouth to work properly so I can tell her I'm fine, but the scream seems to have broken my vocal cords, and I'm real shaky, so even if I were able to say I'm fine, I don't think she'd believe me.

"I heard a scream," Audrey says. "And it didn't sound like a fun scream." She is staring straight at me, and I wonder how she could possibly recognize my voice from a scream. "Kylie, are you okay?"

I nod quickly but tears start filling my eyes and I stay very still so they won't dribble down. I didn't even know I was about to cry. And I don't know why I'm about to cry. But I don't want to look at any of my friends in case they are looking at me like I'm someone they don't want to be around.

Audrey turns her attention to Naomi. "What were y'all doing?"

Naomi takes a small section of her hair and starts twirling it. "Kylie thought she saw a spider, but it was just a shadow." Her voice is calm and steady.

"Is that what happened, Kylie?" Audrey asks me.

I feel like I'm running one of those relay races where runners pass the baton to the next runner. I know

Naomi is handing me a baton, and I'm not supposed to drop it, but I'm not a good liar like she is, and she knows that. I nod carefully, but all the tears that have bubbled up, seep out of my eyes, and I duck my head hoping Audrey won't notice.

"You shouldn't scream if you see a spider," Audrey says sounding distracted and tired. "Spiders in the house are good luck." She looks around the room, her eyes stopping on Naomi, and she gives a small sigh. "Maybe we need more spiders."

I don't know what that's supposed to mean, but I say, "Okay," very softly. I'm not even afraid of spiders and think the study of arachnids is fascinating, but I *am* afraid of people grabbing me and pulling me into a dark, smelly grave.

Audrey goes back upstairs and as soon as she's out of ear shot, Mara starts laughing.

"Gosh, Kylie, you scared me half to death with that scream," she says.

"I *know!*" Nikila says. "You almost gave me a heart attack!" She laughs too as if having a heart attack is so much fun.

Naomi must be sorry she made me sound like a goofball for being freaked out over a spider, because she says, "We don't have to watch the rest if you don't want. It was sort of ridic anyway. If you had been *watching*, you would have known it was all a joke."

Mara nods. "Yeah, the PG-13 ones are sort of silly."

I'm so relieved we aren't going to keep watching the movie I want to cry, but I don't.

We start playing Bucking Bronco, and we all want Nikila to be our horse because she is the best at bucking her rider off. Mara made up the game when we were in second grade and you would think we'd be tired of it by now, but it is still one of our favorite things to do . . . as long as no one else is around.

We are laughing and whinnying and I'm having fun again, but later, when we settle down in our sleeping bags and are whispering in the dark about the party and next year and Cory and how Jessica Stuart was wearing way too short shorts, I start getting nervous.

I keep seeing the face of the girl right before she gets dragged into the hole. And the creepy, scary hands that grabbed her. And how it was not the least bit funny.

One by one, my friends fall asleep. And I'm left alone in the dark.

Sneaky Noises

I flip on my left side and then my right, but I keep thinking about open graves and can't get to sleep.

Suddenly, I have to use the bathroom but I can't make myself get out of my sleeping bag. The room is dark, and I don't want to try to inch my way across all that darkness. I'm sure some pale, scrawny (but strong) hands will grab me before I ever make it to the bathroom.

I remind my body of my experiment and try to explain since everyone is asleep, I have to go to sleep too. But my body argues it can't go to sleep because it really has to pee. If I don't get up soon, I'll have a very soggy sleeping bag and I know that that'll be worse than being dragged into a grave, so I stumble out and run across the room. I remind myself I am a brown belt and if someone tries to grab me, I can kick them really hard.

After I flush, I take my time washing my hands. The foamy hand soap smells like honeydew, or maybe apple and I'm smelling my hands trying to decide which it is when I hear something moving around on the other side of the door. My head tells me it is one of my friends who has to use the bathroom too, but my stomach tells me it is a zombie. Or maybe a whole horde of zombies. Zombies always seem to be in a horde. If I open the door, I will see zombies waiting for me. And I don't think they will get knocked down by a kick. They will grab my leg and start munching on it.

I stand quietly in the bathroom hoping the zombies will get bored and go to another house. I worry the zombies are eating my friends, but then I think, obviously, if zombies were munching on my friends, my friends would be screaming and crying for help, and now all there is on the other side of the door is deadly silence.

This doesn't exactly comfort me.

I pretend my mother is standing there saying, "Enough of this nonsense, Kylie A. Stanton!" because that usually gets me to move, but it doesn't work this time, so I pretend to hear her say, "Aren't you the girl who wanted to do what everybody else was doing? Aren't all your friends on the other side of the door?"

I don't particularly like the tone she's using.

Still, I reach for the doorknob and that's when I hear the noise again. It's a sneaky noise. A noise that can only mean something is moving slowly and quietly across the room. I snatch my hand back.

My heart is beating too fast, and I think I might have to throw up. I hate throwing up.

The air going in and out of my nose must not be reaching my lungs, because even though my nose breaths are extremely loud, I can't breathe. The sneaky noise is getting closer and louder.

I look all around the bathroom but there is no place to hide. It's a tiny room with just a toilet, a sink, and a small cabinet I'm too big to squeeze inside. There is a hand towel hanging next to the sink but that does not seem like a good weapon. I grab it anyway, thinking I could at least snap it at the zombie. And then I pick up the plastic soap dispenser. This is also not a good weapon.

I stare at the doorknob, and I know my eyes are super wide open like Mr. Harold's when he is trying to sing really high notes in music class. I wish I was in music right now. I wish I was anywhere but here. My skin is all goose-bumpy and a thin frosting of sweat is covering my nose.

I know there is something right outside the bathroom door. I try to make my nose breaths come out more quietly, but they are only getting louder and faster. My enormously huge eyes see the doorknob moving the tiniest bit and then the door opens. I shut my eyes and scream and scream and scream. My screams are so loud they tear at my throat.

Hands grab me, and I know I'm going to be pulled into a dark scary hole.

"Kylie! Stop it!"

My eyes jerk open. Naomi is holding me and she looks mad.

"N-Naomi?" I ask, confused.

Before she can answer, heavy footsteps come thundering down the stairs, and Mr. De La Cruz almost runs into Naomi.

"What happened?" he demands. His hair is sticking up and his face looks all puffy.

"I—I—I" is all I can manage to stammer.

Nikila stumbles over with her sleeping bag wrapped around her shoulders. "Kylie, are you *okay*? Why were you screaming?"

Behind her, Mara is sitting up. Her glasses are off and she is squinting trying to see what is going on.

"Are you girls playing some kind of game down here?" Mr. De La Cruz asks sounding angry.

"I just needed to go to the bathroom," Naomi explains. "And *Kylie* was already in there, but I didn't know. And then she started *screaming* at me just because I opened the door." Naomi is acting like I'm the one who did something wrong, even though she was the one who was sneaking around like a zombie.

"I heard something and I . . ." I pause. I set down the soap and rehang the towel. "I got scared," I add in a whisper.

"Kylie, maybe I should call your mom?" Mr. De La Cruz asks.

I swallow and squeeze my index finger. "No, I-I'm okay," I say, but I don't look at Naomi because I'm worried she will be looking at me like, "Please just go home."

Suddenly, Audrey is behind Mr. De La Cruz and she does not look happy. "Daniel, what's going on?"

He doesn't turn around to look at her. "It's fine. I got

it. Go back to bed."

"Doesn't seem like you got it," Audrey says. She peers at me over his shoulder. "You see another spider, Kylie?"

I shake my head. "No."

Audrey looks at the back of Mr. De La Cruz's head, and sighs. "Could you please handle this?" she asks, then she turns around and heads back upstairs. I don't know why Audrey made it sound like this was Mr. De La Cruz's fault when it is clear whose fault this is.

I wish I hadn't screamed.

Mr. De La Cruz stands there for a moment without saying anything, and we are all quiet except for our breaths. Finally, he offers me a small smile. "Let's call it a night, okay? No more screaming?"

I nod. "Sorry," I say.

He puts a hand on my shoulder, then gives Naomi a kiss on the top of her head and makes his way back upstairs.

Naomi and I stand there looking at each other.

"Jeez, Kylie," she says after a while. "You really didn't need to *lose* it like that."

"Why were you being so sneaky?" I ask.

"I was trying to be quiet so I didn't wake up everybody," Naomi says.

"Oh," I say.

Nikila shuffles back to her spot on the floor. I follow her and slide back into my sleeping bag. Naomi goes into the bathroom and shuts the door.

Mara says, "If there *had* been someone down here, I would've tackled them before they got you."

"Thanks," I say and try my best to smile at Mara but it's hard. I lay my head down and close my eyes.

When Naomi comes out of the bathroom, she stomps over to her sleeping bag and loudly rips down the zipper, and I hear her sleeping bag crinkle as she scooches into it. She is breathing loud, and I bet she wants to say something to me, but she doesn't.

"Shhh," Mara tells her, and Naomi tells her to shut it but Mara just laughs.

I wish I could laugh. My whole plan for this summer is to act grown-up, and instead I'm acting like a baby. Nobody else was afraid of the movie, or thought zombies were in the house. I turn so I am facing Naomi. "I'm *really* sorry," I whisper. I can hear tears in my voice, and I shut my eyes again so none can sneak out.

She doesn't say anything for a second but then she whispers back, "It's okay."

Somehow a couple of teardrops escape from my closed eyes, and I wipe them off my arm. It is a super awful thing when the best day of your life ends up being so miserable.

In the morning, Mr. De La Cruz makes us pancakes in odd shapes and wants us to try to guess what they are.

My pancake looks like a big blob, but Mr. De La Cruz insists it is a star.

Mara asks him to make her a volleyball. It just looks like a round pancake, but Mara takes it off her plate, tosses it into the air, and bumps it into her mouth.

No one says anything about me screaming in the middle of the night.

Naomi asks her dad about a hundred times where Audrey is and he shrugs every time until time one hundred and one he says, "Naomi, she didn't tell me where she was going. She's probably at the gym."

Naomi's mouth goes into a straight line, and she doesn't eat any more pancakes even after her dad makes her a perfect N.

Momma comes right after we're done with breakfast. I hate that Naomi seems so grumpy, especially since I'm sure it is my fault, so before I leave, I hug her goodbye and tell her how much fun I had. She hugs me back and says to watch out for any suspicious characters and it's such a Naomi kind of warning that it makes me laugh. I ask her to let me know if she hears anything about everybody going to the beach.

"Dutely, tutely," she says.

Momma waits until we're getting in the car to ask if I had fun and I say, "Of course!" as I slide in and fumble around with my seat belt to avoid looking at her. She didn't ask if I had fun every single second. I *did* have a great time at Cory's party so it's not like I'm lying, but Momma would definitely be able to tell I'm not telling the whole truth if I look right at her. Brianna is in the back seat, and I'm relieved when she yells, "Kylie! Kylie!" as if she hasn't seen me in a month. Momma can't ask any more questions over Brianna's excitement.

I let my sister tell me about all the fun things she has done since yesterday and I make sure to say how much I missed her. I know Momma will think that is very mature and maybe she will stop glancing over at me like she can tell I have been crying.

When we get home, I start to head to my room, but Momma stops me.

"Your sister has been waiting to have some Sparkle time with you," she says, and I know *she* just doesn't want to have to pretend to be a Sparkle Twin.

"I have to do some work on my experiment," I say.

"It's important that I make my scientific observations."

Momma looks at me suspiciously but then she nods, and I dash to my room while Brianna grabs on to Momma's legs.

Although I'm really tired and would rather take a nap than think about my experiment, I take out my notebook. Part of the scientific method is collecting data. You need something to analyze to get to your conclusion.

OBSERVATIONS

> It's good to wear shorts under a dress and maybe this is something that grown people know.
> Being scared that you might die in a trampoline disaster is not babyish.
> Sparkly green toes aren't more grown-up and aren't that pretty.
> Zip lines in backyards are exceptionally cool and it should be a rule that families all have them.
> Crying because you're worried about being eaten by zombies isn't very mature.
> Apologizing to your friend when you have acted immature is very mature.

I tap my pen against my lips and try to analyze the data I have so far. Did I feel grown-up at Cory's? *Mostly* I did. But what about at Naomi's? Definitely not. Sadly, I turn to the last page of my notebook where I drew three boxes. It's my cry chart. This is my most critical piece of data. When I drew the boxes, I hoped I wouldn't have to put a check mark in any of them, all summer.

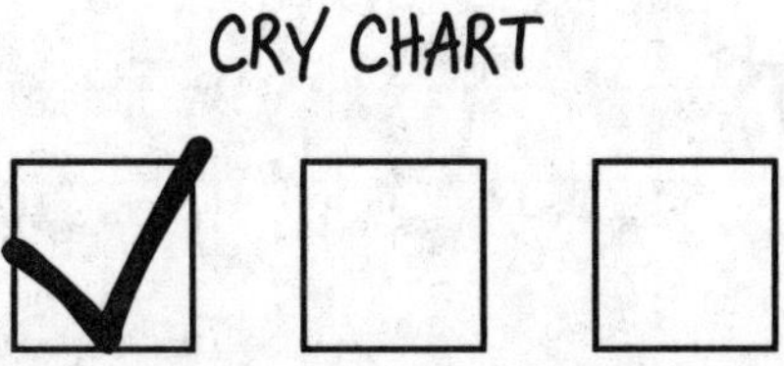

Having to use a check mark when summer just started almost makes me cry. But I don't.

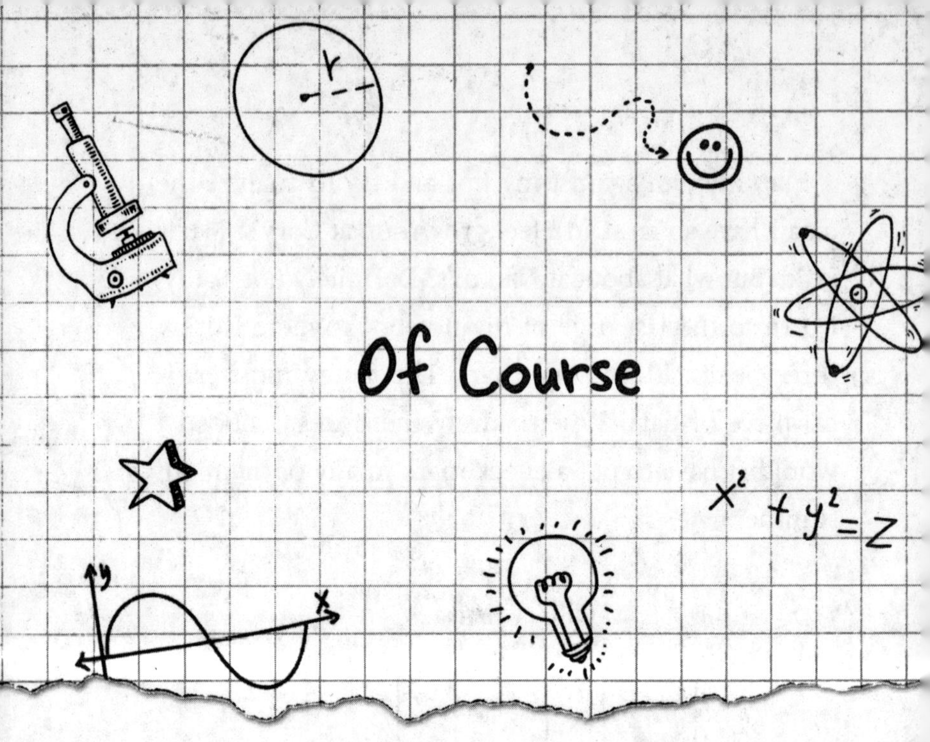

Of Course

The next day, my phone buzzes before I'm even out of bed. It's a message from Mara on our group chat.

I'm glad Mara texted because except for an emoji of a yawning face from Nikila, our chat was completely silent yesterday after we left Naomi's. I have been a little worried it's because they were all mad at me, but Mara's text just says, **What's next?** Followed by a whole string of goofy smiling emojis. I like us going in this direction instead of going backward. Dad likes to say, *Stop looking back, you're not going that way.*

Nikila answers Mara's text right away: **Yes! Let's make**

all the plans! We need to have fun fun fun!!

I'm excited to do the next fun thing too and I'm about to text that but Naomi texts before I can.

First we need to talk about something.

Suddenly, it feels as if someone put a hot heavy blanket on my shoulders. I can see the dots that mean Naomi is texting something else and I'm sure she wants to talk about me acting like a baby and ruining our first big fun thing.

Do you think M&M are secretly undercover agents sent to spy on kids? They were asking me SO many questions at the party. Like why?

That makes me laugh, and I'm relieved that Naomi is being her usual silly self and not mad at me. I text a string of laughing face emojis.

They aren't agents, I text. **Just nosy.**

Were they asking if you're in LOVE with CORY? Mara texts.

Naomi texts back: **NOT EVEN**

Nikila texts a string of skulls that means she's *dying* of laughter.

Naomi texts angry face emojis.

Naomi might be actually annoyed. It's hard to know what will get her mad these days but she has never liked being teased. Mara knows that but doesn't really care. In case Naomi is angry, I start texting about a book I just finished reading. It is about a girl who likes to skateboard and is set in Oakland. I have never read a book where the characters live in a real place right near me.

I loved that book! Nikila texts.

OF COURSE you already read it, Nik! Mara texts.

It feels good to be lying in bed just texting with my friends with no reason to get up and rush around.

Then Mara texts we should go on a bike ride adventure and Naomi texts back that of COURSE Mara would want to do something sporty. Nikila texts that she thinks it would be fun and I laugh out loud when Naomi replies that of COURSE Nikila would say that because she goes along with everything. Naomi isn't being mean. Nikila *is* very agreeable. We all know that about her.

We keep texting silly stuff, but then all of a sudden, a bad feeling washes over me.

No one is talking about how I acted at the sleepover because no one is surprised. Naomi would say of COURSE Kylie got upset and cried. I hate that this is a true thing about me. I want them to think of COURSE Kylie is mature and can handle things and we will be best friends with her forever.

I text, **Whatever you all want to do, I am DOWN!**

Nikila texts, **Me too!**

Naomi texts, **Bet**

And Mara texts that everyone should come over to her house and make plans.

Hopefully, Momma doesn't need me to watch Brianna this morning because I need to get over to Mara's and do whatever my friends are going to do.

There's a whole lot of summer left. No way am I going to be checking any more of those cry boxes.

Not the Only One

Both of Mara's parents are at the hospital where they work, so Momma says I can't go over there and when I put that in the group chat, Naomi asks why did I tell her. Before I can answer, Nikila has already texted that her mom said the same thing.

We end up at Nikila's instead. Going there is really the best because Mrs. Kumar feeds us nonstop. It's like we're there for a party instead of just hanging out.

"Oh, wow, that sauce is spicy!" Mara says, fanning her mouth.

I *like* spicy, so I dip a small piece of warm naan into the red sauce. Immediately my eyes start to water.

"I told you!" Mara says, laughing at me.

We're sitting around the big island in Nikila's kitchen in front of a mountain of snacks. Today there is a big platter of different cheeses and fruit and samosas with the red spicy sauce to dip them in, and tiny tacos and crackers and naan. It's a lot and it is all delicious.

Even though my tongue is burning, I take another scoop of sauce. Tears start streaming down my face and it is strange how much crying from something being spicy makes me laugh. And laughing about it makes me cry even more.

When I did my science experiment about how not to cry when chopping onions, I learned that depending on why you're crying, your tears are made up of different things. I mean all tears are a mix of oil, water, and mucus—which is snot and that is totally gross—but emotional tears have different stuff mixed in. I wonder if that's why the tears that I cry when I'm upset feel so hot.

"Don't cry all over the food!" Naomi squeals and Mara pretends to dribble tears onto the platter.

"Yummy! Tear seasoning!" Nikila says, and shovels food into her mouth. The hot sauce doesn't make her eyes water even a little. "And this is *so* not spicy." She smacks her lips.

We go back to talking about ideas for summer plans, but Naomi keeps saying everything is boring. So far, the library summer reading game is boring, the Rodin sculptures at Stanford are boring, watching the skydivers in Pacifica is boring, and so is trying to make the longest gum wrapper chain.

"What *isn't* boring, then?" Mara asks. "You can't shoot *everything* down."

"I don't know," Naomi says. "But we've done all those things."

"Not the gum wrapper chain," Nikila argues. The chain was her idea, and I don't want to hurt her feelings, but I really don't want to sit inside folding small pieces of paper all summer.

Mrs. Kumar is flitting around, cleaning dishes and rearranging pots. She provides a few suggestions: arranging our closets, going to the Tech museum, volunteering at a Bay cleanup. Her ideas aren't any worse than ours, but each time she offers a suggestion, Nikila says, "Mom, please stop."

Mr. Kumar comes into the kitchen and goes straight to the food. "Oh, yum!" he says.

"Shoo, you!" Mrs. Kumar says and snaps a kitchen towel at him. "That's for the girls."

"But my belly needs attention too," Mr. Kumar says

and rubs his stomach. He puts an entire samosa in his mouth and his eyes bulge while he chews and tries to swallow it down. "Oh, my love," he tells Mrs. Kumar. "I will adore you until the stars fall from the sky as long as you keep cooking like that."

"Get out, Dad!" Nikila shouts at him.

Naomi stands up suddenly. "I have to go to the bathroom."

"Get out of here," Mrs. Kumar tells her husband, but she doesn't sound truly angry. As he leaves, he grabs one more samosa and gives us a sneaky look.

When Naomi comes back into the kitchen, she looks grumpy. Maybe the spicy food isn't agreeing with her.

Mrs. Kumar leans against the island and smiles at us. "Mara is still the only one who's gotten her period?" she asks and I almost spit out a clump of cheese.

"Mo-om!" Nikila shouts.

"What? What?" she asks, sounding just like I did when I asked about Naomi's bra.

It's sort of funny but Mara's cheeks have gotten red, and she shoves a big piece of naan into her mouth. Naomi picks up a piece of naan too, but she doesn't eat it, she just starts tearing it into pieces.

"We're all women here, no?" Mrs. Kumar says, ignoring Nikila's horrified look.

"Mara's not the only one. I got mine too," Naomi says.

My mouth drops open because this news is too big for me to just be hearing about it. "*When?*" I ask.

"Really?" Mara asks. "It's gross, right?"

"Gross?" Mrs. Kumar repeats. "Not a bit. Simple biology."

I suppose as a scientist I should be agreeing with Mrs. Kumar but I am more concerned about getting left behind.

"When Nikila starts, I'll give her a beautiful sari to celebrate. If we were back home, all of her aunties would make such a fuss," Mrs. Kumar says.

"Good thing we're not in India, then," Nikila mutters and her mom gives her a stern look. "Sor-ry," Nikila says.

I notice Naomi never answered me, so I repeat my question. "When did you start?"

"Oh my gosh!" she says, sounding annoyed. "It's *private*. Everyone knows that, Kylie!"

I have said the wrong thing again. I should've noticed that neither Mara or Nikila asked that. But it's tiring trying to focus on always doing and saying the right thing. My head starts to hurt and my throat gets tight. It doesn't seem like my experiment is helping me at all. Any second a gush of tears is going to come right out.

Nikila must sense that things are going wrong because she jumps up and claps her hands. "Oh my gosh! You have to hear my rendition of 'Lavender Blue'!"

"You can't play them 'Morning Mood'?" Mrs. Kumar asks but then she waves her question away. "I know, I know, what am I thinking that you ladies would want a little classical." She sighs like it's so tragic that we'd rather hear something fast and current instead of from a million years ago.

We follow Nikila to the Kumar's family room where there's an upright piano pressed against the wall and Nikila sits down and does a whole fakey finger stretch and then she begins to play.

She's really good. And Mara starts dancing and then Naomi grabs my hands and makes me dance with her and I guess that's almost like her saying she's sorry she snapped at me. It takes a few minutes but pretty soon, I've danced away the bad feeling and wanting to cry about it.

Later, when I'm back home, I ask Brianna if she wants to play Sparkle Twins. She's surprised because it's never me that suggests we play her favorite thing.

"Yay!" she yells and gives me a hug.

I don't tell Brianna that sometimes (a lot of times), it's fun to pretend to be a Sparkle Twin because she never makes me feel like I do everything wrong.

OBSERVATIONS

> Your friends can be wrong about you.
> I thought best friends should tell each other everything. Even if it is private. But I am not telling my friends about my experiment.

Now it's just me and Nikila who haven't gotten our periods. What if Nikila gets hers this summer? Then it will just be me. The oddball. That seems just as bad as a crybaby.

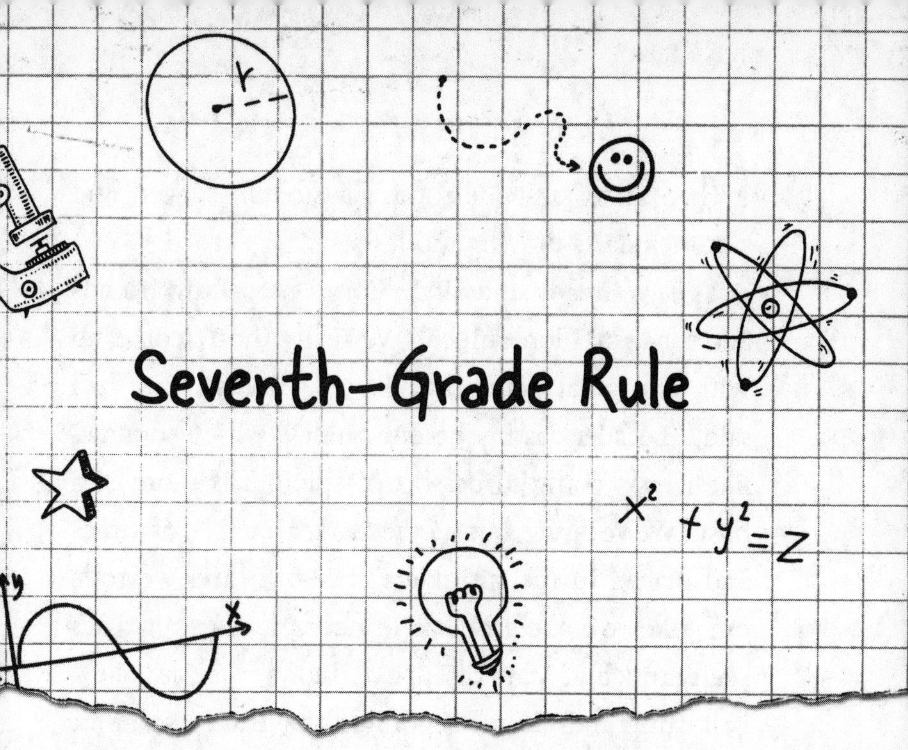

Seventh-Grade Rule

At the beginning of summer vacation, time feels like it's moving in slow motion. It's like taking one of those huge cat stretches in bed, where your toes almost reach the door and your fingers could be out the window.

Dad is gone again, and this is another really long trip all through Europe. Momma, Brianna, and I miss him, but during the summer it's hard to keep track of how long he will be gone.

For days, I wake up late, stay in my pj's for as long as I want, watch silly videos with Brianna, have pancakes for lunch, and paint my nails different wild colors (but not green).

Then all of a sudden, the cat stretch is over, and summer starts moving too fast.

It's *July* already and since Cory's party, my friends and I haven't done much. We really didn't come up with any great plans that day at Nikila's. Mara had said, "Let's let destiny be our guide!" which sounded like it was going to be sort of epic but is more of a bust. We've hung out at the park a couple of times and played in the sprinklers at Mara's, and we rode our bikes over to Douglas to check it out, but that's pretty much it. Mara disappeared for a week at volleyball camp and Naomi is going to be leaving soon for drama camp. I'm beginning to wonder if my great big experiment is going to be one great big flop.

My phone lights up with a message in our group chat. It's Naomi.

Julie texted me. Everybody is going to the beach TODAY! 😊😊😊😊😊☼☼☼☼☼

Mara texts back immediately: **Yaaaaaassss!**

Nikila: **Awesome!!**

And I can totally see her big grin. I get tingly with excitement. *Finally*! I send a thumbs-up emoji.

I'm so relieved I can get back to my experiment. It's hard to know if you're becoming mature when you aren't really *doing* anything.

I go to our guest bedroom. Since we don't have overnight company that often, Momma uses the room as her office. When the door is closed, we aren't supposed to go in there because she is either teaching one of her remote classes or studying. It seems funny to me that Momma is a teacher *and* a student. It doesn't seem like you can be both at the same time, but she says that's how it is when you're working to get your PhD.

I'm relieved to see the door is open, so it is okay to bother her. As soon as I get in the room, I say, "Hi, Momma. I'm going to go to the beach today." As the words come out, they don't feel right, and I see Momma's shoulders tense up and her fingers pause on her keyboard. Maybe it would have been better to *ask* if I could go.

"The beach?" Momma asks, as if she's never heard of such a place, and she goes back to *tap tap tapping* on her keyboard. "Who's going?"

"*Everybody*, Momma," I say.

She turns away from her computer and leans her chin into her hand.

Brianna, who was lying underneath Momma's desk, springs up. "The beach?" she cries. "I wanna go!" Then she holds her hands out like paws, sticks her tongue out, and pants.

I shake my head at her. "This is just for kids my age. It's like a school party."

"But it's summer!" Brianna shouts, like I'm playing a dirty trick on her. She forgets about being a puppy and juts her chin out in a pout. "You can't have a school party in the summer, can you, Momma?"

Before Momma can answer, I try to make Brianna understand. "You are *so* right, Bree. I shouldn't have said a *school* party. I should have said a *seventh*-grade party, and since you're not in seventh grade . . ." I let my voice just trail off, and give a little shrug to say, it's not even my rule, it's the seventh-grade-beach-party rule, so what can I do?

"But you're not in seventh grade either," Brianna complains. She climbs out from under the desk and faces me with her hands on her hips. "You shouldn't get to do seventh-grade things."

It feels like Brianna punched me in my belly. "Yes, I *am*," I say, putting my hands on my hips and not looking at Momma. "As soon as you promote out of sixth, you're in seventh and you get to do all the things that are for seventh graders."

"I don't know about the beach, Kylie," Momma says. "I have a lot of work to get done today. I was counting on you to watch Brianna."

"I don't need to be watched, Momma," Brianna says, sounding insulted.

Just last week, Brianna decided she wanted to bake cookies and got a bowl and dumped a whole bag of chocolate chips and all the sugar that was in the sugar bowl into it. She added a clump of margarine but couldn't reach the flour. She added some water and stirred it and put watery clumps on a cookie sheet and put it in the oven. When the smoke alarm started going off and Momma found the forgotten cookie sheet in the oven, she was not happy. Brianna *definitely* needs to be watched.

I know Dad traveling all the time makes things harder for Momma, but I don't think it's fair for her to expect me to babysit Brianna as if I don't have my own life to lead.

"But *everybody's* going," I repeat. It's the only ammunition I have.

Momma winks at my sister. "We *like* to watch you. You do amazing things."

Brianna crosses her arms over her chest and stands taller. "If you go to the beach without me, Kylie, you will miss all my amazing things."

"You can tell me about them when I get back," I say to her.

"Okay." Brianna nods solemnly.

"So," I say, turning back to Momma. "I can go, right?"

Brianna has lost interest in this conversation now that she knows she isn't going and starts gathering markers and construction paper and glue.

"Even if everybody is going, I'm not comfortable if there isn't going to be supervision. I don't like the idea of a bunch of kids hanging out at the beach with no adults around. There are no lifeguards there."

Momma is making it sound like the beach is a dangerous place, when it isn't. It's not even a real beach. There's no waves or seashells or anything; it's just a small strip of sand next to the Bay. I know Momma doesn't think it's dangerous. She likes to jog there on weekend mornings. And sometimes she lets Brianna and me walk along the water while she sits and reads on a towel. The air smells fresh and clean, and not at all like the stinky egg smell you get way down by the Dumbarton Bridge.

"I'll find out if a parent is going, okay?" I leave the room to text in private because I don't want Momma to see my face if Naomi tells me I'm ridic for thinking a parent would be there.

But as it turns out, Audrey was planning on going

all along; I don't know why Naomi didn't just say that from the beginning. Then Naomi texts:

And shave that fringe off your legs! After that there's about a million laughing-so-hard-you're-crying emojis.

I feel hot all over, like I have a bad fever. I turn my phone over so I don't have to see those laughing faces.

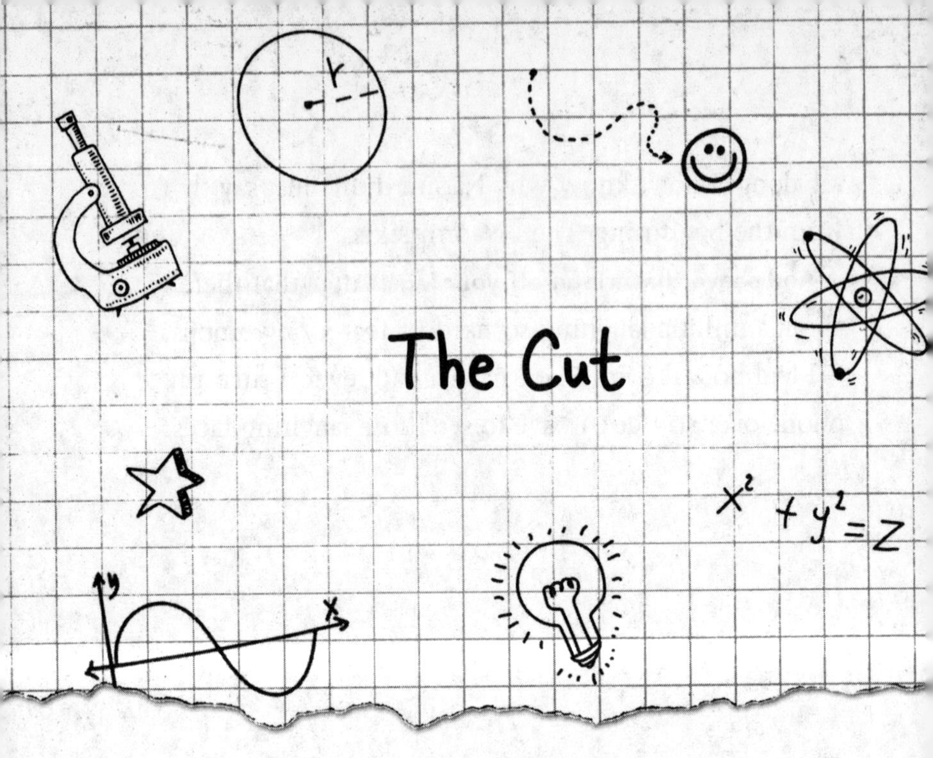

The Cut

I'm the only one of my friends who doesn't shave their legs. And I had hoped no one had noticed. I'm pretty brown-skinned, so I thought maybe the hair kind of just blended in, but Naomi calling it fringe makes it clear that not only does my hair not blend in, even *worse*, I have bushy *bear* legs. Momma has had this *issue* about me not shaving my legs, claiming I'm too young. But if I'm too young, then why does every other girl my age get to?

When I go back to talk to Momma, I see Brianna has started the beginning of a castle in the corner of the room. She has taped construction paper together and cut out windows and drawn designs on the paper to make it look like bricks and ivy.

"Audr— I mean, Mrs. De La Cruz is going," I say.

Momma rests her fingers on her computer keys and stares at the screen for a moment. "I guess that should be fine, then," she says, even though it doesn't sound like she thinks it is fine.

I twist my hands together, afraid to ask what I want to. "Momma," I start. "You know how it is so majorly important when you're doing an experiment to make sure you stick to all the rules?"

"Mm-hmm," Momma says, looking at her computer as if she's not really listening to me.

"So," I say. I start to lose my nerve a little, but I clear my throat and go on. "So, really, since all the other girls are shaving their legs, I need to also." I quickly look down at the carpet so Momma can't see the small smile tickling my mouth.

"Shave?" Brianna says. "Like Daddy?"

Quickly, I look back up. "No!" I say. "Not like Daddy, like Momma." Brianna is being too silly. "I don't have a beard."

Brianna looks at Momma and her eyes get wide and anxious. "You shave yourself, Momma?"

For some reason, I find this hilarious and start

laughing. Momma doesn't seem amused at all. In fact, she looks annoyed. I stop laughing. Maybe this was supposed to be secret. "It's no big deal, Bree," I say.

"Is it ouchie?" Brianna asks, her voice just above a whisper.

"No, Baby B," Momma says and flashes me an exasperated look. "And it's not something you need to think about." She doesn't even look at me when she adds, "Use the pink ones, not the blue."

It's like she is talking in code, like we're secret agents or something. "Okay, thanks," I say, hardly able to contain my excitement. I walk out the room slowly to show how mature I am but as soon as I'm in the hallway, I run to the closet where we keep all the extra supplies like lotion and soap and toilet paper. There is a pack of blue razors that Dad uses, and a pack of pink ones that are Momma's. I grab a pink one and head to my parents' bathroom to get shaving cream.

Spraying on shaving cream is fun. It's smooth and fluffy just like whipped cream. When the razor slides through it, it reminds me of a snowplow cutting through drifts of snow. I clear one road, then another.

I don't even feel the cut. The only reason I know something has happened is when the shaving cream turns from creamy white, to pink, to red. This isn't good. I thought I was being extra super careful. It seems very strange my leg doesn't hurt, but as I watch the patch of red foam get bigger and bigger, my leg starts to sting, and that hurts. A lot. "Ow, ow, ow!" I cry out.

"Kylie?" Momma calls, and then she comes into the bathroom. I'm so relieved she doesn't get mad, just worried. "Oh, baby, that must sting," she says, and she takes the razor from my hand. "I don't know what I was thinking . . ." Her voice trails off.

I can tell she is thinking this is her fault. "It's okay, Momma," I say really fast even though tears are in my eyes. "It hardly hurts anymore." This isn't true at all.

"Let's get that shaving cream off, okay?" She asks and grabs a hand towel. After running it under some cold water, she washes off my leg.

I had hoped once the cream was gone, my leg would stop stinging, but it doesn't stop, and now I can see a small pink line snaking down my leg, filling back up with blood. This makes me start crying for real.

"It's really shallow. Don't worry." Momma's voice is soft and gentle, the way she talks to me when I have had a nightmare. She puts some toilet tissue on the cut, and it sticks to my leg.

Sometimes, when my dad is home, he comes out of

the bathroom and has small pieces of tissue stuck to his face. It looks so silly. By the time I stop thinking about that, I realize my leg doesn't hurt anymore. I look down and notice I have one smooth hairless leg and one hairy one. I'm not sure if I like this whole shaving thing. Momma puts her hand on my shoulder.

"You want me to shave the other one?" she asks, and I nod.

As Momma shaves my leg, she explains about how not to press too hard and shows me how to do long, even strokes. She tells me knees are tricky and that's why she usually just stops below her knees. I have never noticed that before, but Momma pulls her robe up and I see she does have a little bit of hair on her thighs.

"You know, the first time I shaved my legs, I snuck and did it even though Big Mama had said no." Momma was raised by her grandmother because her mom got really sick and died when Momma was little. She barely even remembers her mom. Big Mama is very strict and has a fancy room in her house that Brianna and I aren't even allowed to go into.

"Did you get in trouble?" I ask.

"Oh, you know I did!" Momma says. "Big Mama swatted my behind with her hairbrush and didn't care that I had cut myself. Said it served me right." Momma laughs as if this is almost a happy memory. It sounds horrible to me. Momma and Dad never hit me or Brianna. They say talking to us when we do something wrong is better because we need to learn instead of being scared of them. Even though they don't hit us, I'm still scared of getting in trouble. Getting *talked to* can feel pretty awful.

"Don't try to grow up too fast," Momma says and gives me a side hug and even though her hug feels good, I worry about what she said.

"But I have to grow up, Momma," I say.

"I know," she says with a little sigh. Then she wipes her hands together and heads out of the bathroom. "Stay where Mrs. De La Cruz can see you. And make sure to put on sunscreen," she tosses over her shoulder.

By the time I am ready for the beach, I have two smooth legs and the bloody tissue is in the trash. You can see a small nick where I cut myself, but otherwise, my legs look great without all that hair. And they aren't a bit ashy, because I sprayed them good with the sunscreen and now my legs are smooth and glossy.

I hear the *beep, beep* of Audrey's car horn and grab my bag.

Momma just waves at Audrey from the front door. She's still in her robe so she doesn't want to go outside.

Nikila and Mara are making silly faces at me and Naomi hollers, "Come on, Kylie!"

I give Momma a hug and dash to the car. I've never been this excited to go to the beach.

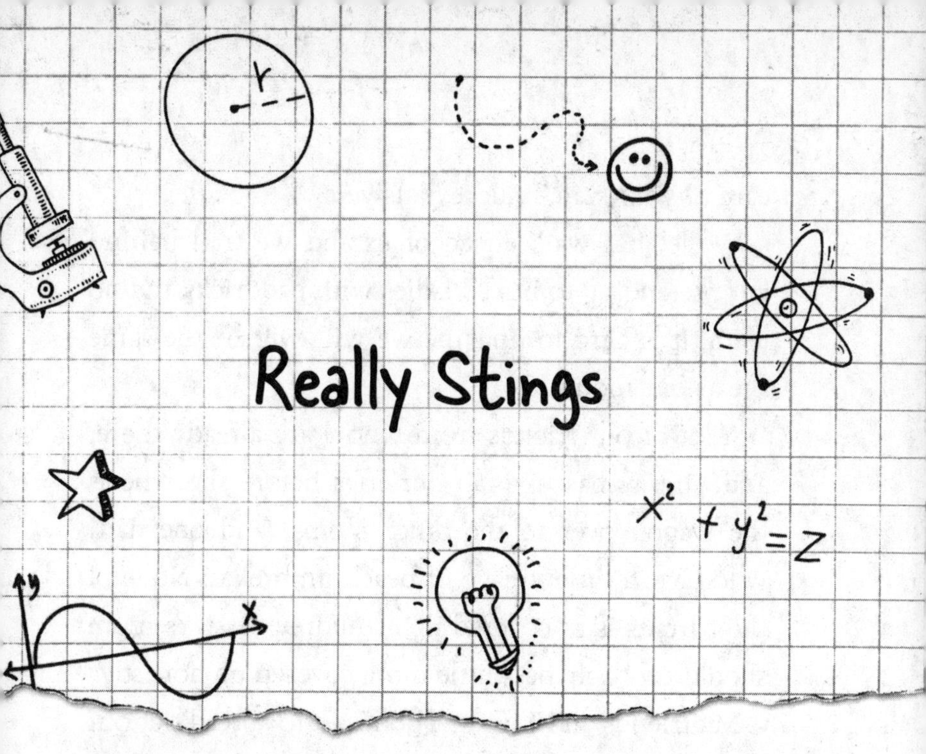

Really Stings

We're ready to race to the sand as soon as Audrey parks, but first we have to pile the cooler, all our bags, a sand chair, and a beach umbrella into the red wagon that's always in the trunk. After we're done loading up, Audrey pops a ginormous black straw hat on her head.

"Really, Mom?" Naomi asks and rolls her eyes.

Audrey is wearing a long-sleeve shirt and wide flowy pants. It does not really look like a beach outfit.

"You could just stay under the umbrella," Naomi tells her.

"When you're my age, you'll wish you had taken

care of your skin," Audrey answers.

We let her walk ahead of us and we trail behind her pretending to be old ladies with bad backs and no teeth. It is hard to imagine we will ever be the same age as our moms.

A lot of our friends from school are already there, and Audrey has us grab our bags before she wheels the wagon over to the other moms (and one dad) who have a little village of beach umbrellas. None of the parents is as covered up as Audrey. Jessica's mom should probably be a little more covered up honestly.

My friends and I find a good spot to spread out our towels. Close to everyone, but also with some space so it's just us. We let our towels overlap so we have made our own large square and use our sandals on the corners. Getting things set up perfectly has us all hot and sweaty and we peel off our shorts and tops and Nikila gives us spritzes from a small spray bottle of water.

I normally don't wear a two-piece because it just feels like way too much skin out there, but Naomi had declared one-piece suits "babyish" at the beginning of the summer and Nikila and Mara had agreed. Since my friends were all wearing two-pieces, so am I.

"Cover those things," Naomi tells Mara, making fun of Mara's boobs.

I think Naomi is just jealous because she is tired of being flat like me, but Mara turns bright red and yanks her top back on.

Mara doesn't get embarrassed easily and seeing her not feel good about herself makes me mad.

"Don't be a jerk," I tell Naomi.

Naomi's eyes get a little wide, but then they narrow and she puts her hands on hips. "Or what?" she says leaning toward me.

My chest starts thumping like a drum. I take some deep breaths to try to slow my heartbeat. I don't want to get in a big argument, but Mara always stands up for us, so I need to have her back. "You're being mean." I don't add that as a matter of fact, she is being mean a lot lately.

Nikila looks back and forth between us. "Guys?" she asks like she can't understand what is happening.

"It's whatever," Mara says. "No biggie."

Naomi snickers over the word *biggie*, and I expect her to double down and say something worse, but then she just starts laughing like a donkey. "For real? Can't you take a joke?" She juts her hip at Mara. "Mara knows I was just kidding!"

Mara shakes her head and looks up at the sky like Naomi is a bratty kid she has to deal with. "I wasn't worried about it," she says but she doesn't take her T-shirt back off.

It's like a dark cloud settled over us for a minute but then the breeze from the Bay blows it away and we start laughing at how Ashanté Miller's mom is chasing her with a bottle of sunscreen.

We plow through a bag of barbecue chips that seem even saltier than normal and slurp down juice boxes (which is probably not very grown-up of us, but none of us are ready to give up strawberry kiwi goodness). Cory walks by and kicks some sand on Naomi's towel and she calls him a jerk, but she is laughing when she says it and her eyes follow him as he wanders through the crowd of towels. Cory was already popular, but after his party it is like everyone is his best friend and he is like a bee gathering pollen, stopping at one group of kids and then another and making everyone laugh. (I have all sorts of questions about bees and I'd like to do science project on them, but I'm too afraid of getting stung.)

The sun is really baking us, and I try to get comfortable on my towel but lying in the sun isn't really my thing and I want to go into the water. "Come on!" I say, springing up. "Let's go in!" I fill my voice with a ton of enthusiasm so they will agree that going into the water is more fun than trying to turn into a sun-dried tomato. Some of the other kids pop up and without even waiting for me, start running to the water. That's cool, but I need Group A to go in.

Mara looks over at Naomi, and then she slowly pulls her T-shirt off. Then she sets her glasses on top of it and stands. "Okay, let's go," she says.

I'm so glad. All I needed was for not *all* of them to lie there.

The small strip of sand is hot as I run across it and I don't even stop to check the water temperature, I run right in. But when I get just up to my knees, I dash back out.

"Ow, ow, ow!" My legs are stinging like crazy. I look down, sure there must be a million baby jellyfish attached to me, but there is nothing.

Mara squints at my legs. "Did you shave?" she asks, and I nod, not knowing what that has to do with the hard pinches on my legs. "You should always shave the day before you go to the beach," she explains. "Otherwise, it really stings when you go into the salt water."

Why doesn't anybody ever tell me these things? I wonder. That would have been some real handy information to know. "I'll remember that," I tell Mara, and then I add, "You look great in your bikini." This is the truth but I also want to make sure she doesn't feel bad about herself. "Naomi is just jealous."

Mara smiles at me. "Thanks," she says. "And don't worry about your legs. It just stings for a minute and then you'll be okay."

Mara has never lied to me, so I dash back in. Mara follows me, and we start screaming and splashing and she's right, because after a minute, my legs aren't bothering me at all.

Naomi and Nikila join us in the water and Naomi hits Mara with a big splash.

"Got you!" she crows. I like the days when Naomi doesn't straighten her hair and she isn't worried about getting it wet.

Mara hits Naomi with an even bigger splash. "Got you back!"

Naomi shrieks and then dives under the water like a mermaid. When she pops back up, she grabs Mara around the waist. "Sorry, Mara. You look awesome."

This is the Naomi I'm used to. Quick with a tease but just as quick with an apology.

Mara says, "You didn't bother me! I just don't want everyone to realize I'm secretly from Themyscira!" She holds her arms up. "Amazons forever!"

We all laugh at that and talk about how cool it would be to live on the island with Wonder Woman and her Amazon sisters.

It's a perfect day. The sun is shining down bright and hot, making the cold water feel great, and everyone is laughing and jostling around and having fun.

When I get home, I'll be able to write about how I'm proving my hypothesis. Doing what everyone is doing is the best.

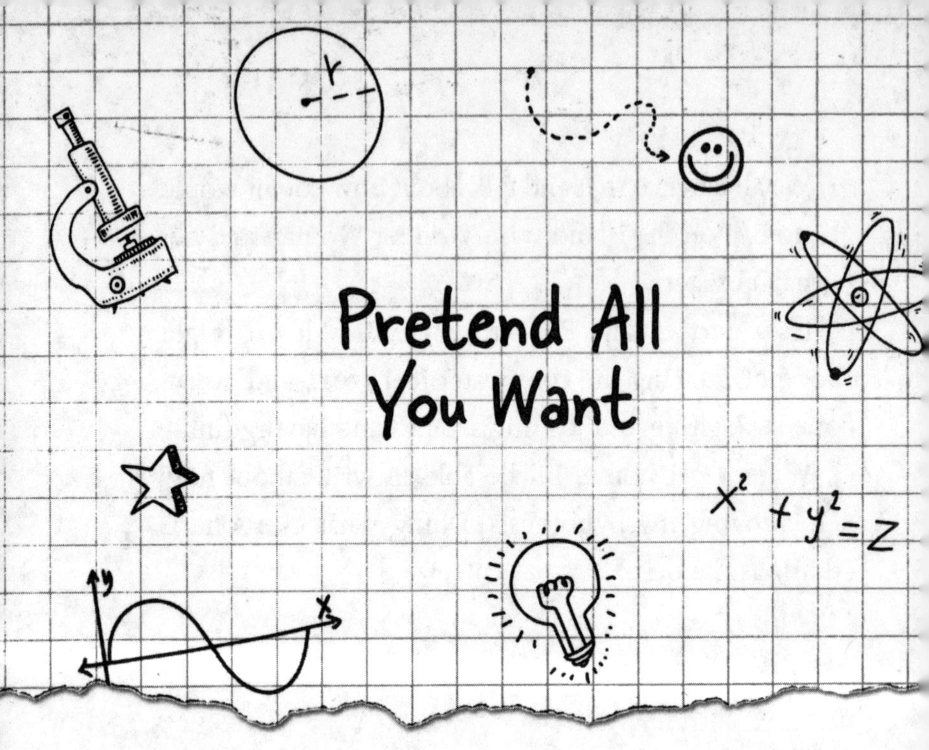

Pretend All You Want

Naomi keeps nudging us to move farther and farther down the beach even though Audrey had warned us we had to stay right near her big red umbrella so we'd be in sight of her and the other parents. I know Naomi is embarrassed by what her mother is wearing and doesn't want to be associated with her. I honestly can't blame her. Considering it is over eighty degrees, Audrey looks very odd all covered up.

"She wanted me to wear a *visor* today," Naomi says, shuddering.

Nikila nods solemnly. "My mom slathered me with so much sunscreen this morning our whole house smelled like a coconut."

Suddenly, I get hit by a big splash of water, right in my face, and by the time I stop coughing and wiping my eyes, I see a bunch of boys laughing while they try to swim away.

"Get 'em!" I shout and we take off after them, struggling to run through the water.

By the time we catch them, everybody else has gotten into the water and we start a majorly huge water fight. It's awesome.

Although there's a ton of splashing going on, I can't help noticing Cory is only splashing Naomi, and she keeps splashing him back.

Naomi can pretend all she wants, but they obviously like each other. Maybe he will ask her to be his girlfriend. If he does, she will be the only one in our group with a boyfriend. I'm okay with that. I wouldn't want to be first. If Naomi is first, then we can ask her questions, like, do your hands get all sweaty when you're holding his and what's it like kissing a real person instead of a pillow, and whether she is in love. Stuff like that.

Audrey hollers it's lunchtime and we all scamper out of the water and head over like hungry wolves. All of us except Naomi and Cory. I'm worried Naomi won't come because of her mom's outfit, and I turn around to tell her not to be silly, and that's when I see

Cory lean over and get really close to Naomi, and her lean toward him and then they kiss!

I say, "Oh!" because I'm so surprised and I turn back around quick. It's like I just opened the bathroom stall door on someone. I hurry over to get some food, but I can't wait to get all the details from Naomi. A minute later, she is right next to me, looking like nothing at all happened.

"Wow," I whisper to her. "What was it like?"

"What are you talking about?" she asks and grabs some chips and a soda. She goes and sits on her towel, next to Nikila and Mara, and I get a sandwich and an apple and then I follow her. I know I made a mistake. I should've waited until it was just our group to say something. She wouldn't want just anybody to know her business.

When I sit down on my towel, Naomi sort of glares at me.

"I'm sorry," I say. "Me and my big mouth, right?" I smile at her to let her know I know I messed up. But now it's just us. "So," I say, lowering my voice. "Is he a good kisser?"

Naomi shoots me an angry look. "Stop messing around, Kylie."

Now I'm confused. "I *saw* you," I say.

"What?" Nikila asks. "What did you see?"

"She didn't see *anything*," Naomi says, and she says it tightly, like it hurts her to move her mouth, so I don't argue.

But I stare at her until she looks away.

I don't understand. I saw them kiss. I don't know why she'd lie about it.

Mara looks at both of us. "I think Kylie did see something," she says. "Or at least she thinks she did." She leans toward me and lowers her voice. "What do you think you saw?"

Nikila giggles but it's not her usual happy sound. "It's so hot! Maybe we should go back in the water?"

I'm sure Nikila can feel a storm brewing and is trying to avoid it.

I don't know what I should say. Maybe Naomi is trying to tell me it is none of my business. And that hurts because I thought friends shared everything. What is going on with Naomi? I ignore Nikila and say, "I *thought* I saw Cory and Naomi kiss."

Nikila gasps and Mara says, "What?" really loud. Naomi's face gets stormy and she glares at me.

"But I guess I didn't," I hurriedly say. It's the best I can do, and I hope Naomi realizes I'm making a big sacrifice here.

"I told her we didn't," Naomi says, like there is something wrong with me for believing my own eyes. But she didn't tell me that and I don't know why she sounds so angry.

"You *really* didn't?" Mara asks Naomi.

Naomi doesn't even hesitate. "No!"

I count Naomi's lies in my head:

She lied about me not seeing anything.
+ She lied about telling me they didn't kiss.
+ She lied about them kissing.

= 3 lies

Three lies seem like a lot. Friends aren't supposed to lie to each other. As much as I know Naomi lies about stuff, for some reason I didn't think she'd lie to me.

"I think you did," Mara says to Naomi. "Because if you didn't, why would you be so mad?"

Naomi stands up. "If you were my friends, you'd believe *me*." Then she walks away.

It's weird the way she said that. Like she was saying they should believe her *over* me. My eyes narrow as I watch Naomi leave our group.

"Did you really see them kiss?" Nikila asks.

I watch Naomi perch on the edge of Julie's towel (which is very far from Cory's) and laugh at something, and I feel all strange inside. Sort of like crying and a little bit like hitting something. "I . . . I don't know what I saw," I finally say.

"You should be careful with stuff like that," Nikila says. She gets up and dusts sand off her legs and then she goes and sits with Naomi.

Everything feels upside down. For at least half a minute I think that maybe I didn't really see what I thought. And that makes my head hurt.

"I believe you," Mara says.

Maybe that should make me feel better, but it doesn't. I don't want it to be me and Mara against Nikila and Naomi, but that's what it feels like. The whole point of my experiment is to make sure the four of us stick together. I don't know what to do. I look across the group of kids until I find Cory. He is sitting and laughing with some other boys, and I wonder what is so funny and I sure hope that it isn't anything about kissing.

After lunch, I notice how Naomi makes a point of keeping away from Cory, and that makes me think the only reason Naomi lied was because she must be really super embarrassed.

Like when I let loose a really big stink in class last year and then moved my desk away from Marla Kander so everyone would think it was her. Everyone *did* think it was her and teased her and no one would believe her when she kept saying it wasn't. I laughed right along with everybody and even said "Methinks she protests too much." I knew it was mean, but I was so relieved no one knew I had farted.

So Cory and Naomi kissing is *probably* like that. She couldn't help herself from lying about it, because the kiss makes her feel bad. Maybe it was awful. Or maybe she is worried that we would think she shouldn't have done it. And maybe a mature friend wouldn't have said anything about what they saw. But it was just a kiss.

For a little while it feels like Mara and I are on one side of a fence and Nikila and Naomi are on the other, but when somebody says we should build the biggest sandcastle ever and we all are digging moats and dumping piles of wet sand, whatever fence was there seems to be mostly knocked down.

Still, we're sort of quiet on the ride home, and when Audrey drops me off I say, "Bye, Naomi," really sweetly.

"Bye," she says quietly, but then she gives me a lopsided smile. "See ya."

“Dutely, tutely,” I say, which cracks her up and just like that, we’re fine.

OBSERVATIONS

- If you cut yourself shaving it hurts. (And even if you don’t cut yourself, your skin will sting if you go into salty water.)
- As we get older, we get hair in places we didn’t used to, and to show we’re older . . . we shave it off. At least that’s true if you’re a girl. Sort of strange if you ask me.
- Sometimes I think things were better when me and my friends could act silly and be more relaxed.

I pause for a moment thinking about all the other observations I have about today and what it might mean for my experiment. At least my disagreement with Naomi didn’t make me cry, but it did make me feel awful. And confused. Finally I write the one thing I think is true.

- There’s nothing mature about lying.

Don't Say It

Brianna and I are going to see the Sparkle Twins movie today. Commercials for the movie have been playing for weeks, and Brianna has been so excited for opening day she's been a little impossible. She keeps wanting me to reread all the Sparkle Magic books to her and pretend we are Luna and Lena, the Sparkle elf twins. When we play, I have to let her be Luna. Luna is the funny one and always wears a sparkly tutu. Lena is the smart one and sort of sarcastic so honestly, Brianna and I are well-suited for the parts we play. Sometimes when we get really into being the twins, I forget I'm much older than Brianna. I can almost believe we truly are twins.

My friends think G-rated movies are for babies, so I don't invite them. Besides, the Sparkle Twins are really Brianna's and my thing.

It's when we are standing in line to get our oversized tub of popcorn that I see them.

Mara, Naomi, and Nikila. They are standing in line for a movie. They are standing in line for a movie they are going to see without me.

For a quick moment, I try to make myself believe they called me to come too, or I didn't see a text. But I know that's not true. Still, I pull out my phone and check. Nope. No text. Or missed call.

I don't want them to see me, but Brianna doesn't know that, and so when she sees them too, she shouts, "Hi, Nik! Hi, Naomi! Mara, hi!" She waves and jumps up and down like they might not see her.

The three of them turn toward us, and now they all look like bugs stuck in the middle of a hungry spider's web.

While Momma pays for the popcorn, I slowly walk toward my friends, who are slowly walking toward me.

"I didn't know you were going to the movies," I say. My voice sounds shaky, and I don't know what's wrong with my throat, but it feels like it got smaller.

Nikila is the one who starts explaining, and she talks so fast, it's hard to keep up. "We're seeing *Rain*, you know that creepy movie with the people who come out of raindrops and get you and it's supposed to be totally scary, and we knew you didn't like movies like that because of the last time. Remember the whole thing at Naomi's? And we didn't want you to feel bad like you would feel you had to come or something when obviously you don't like to be scared, even though I think it's fun and so does Naomi and Mara, but it's okay you don't, and you shouldn't feel bad we came because we only wanted to make sure you didn't feel left out."

Blurting all that makes her breathe hard, and Naomi and Mara are nodding like bobblehead dolls, as if Nikila is making so much sense.

"You still could've asked me," I say in a low voice, as I lean back on my heels and then up on my toes, back and forth, back and forth, like my friends are turning the rope and I'm trying to jump in. Nikila must've said they didn't want me to feel bad like thirty times in her little speech. That's what Momma would call irony.

"But you wouldn't have wanted to come," Naomi says, like I am being illogical.

"Right?" Mara asks, and that makes me mad because I feel like she wants me to agree that they shouldn't have asked me.

Momma walks over with Brianna. "Hi, girls," she says to my friends. Then she looks over their heads and around. "You're here by yourself?"

"Hi, Mrs. Stanton," they all chime together.

"My mom dropped us off," Naomi says.

Nikila looks over at her with an odd expression and I wonder what that's about. I want to ask what the deal is, but I don't think I can say anything right now without my voice sounding mean.

Momma must not think it's a big deal they don't have a parent with them because she just smiles and then turns to me. "Let's go, Ky, the movie is going to start."

"What movie are you here to see?" Mara asks.

I try to use telepathy. *Don't say it!* I beam to Brianna. *Don't!* I beam to Momma. It is bad enough that my friends didn't include me in their plans, but for them to find out I'm here to see a G-rated movie?

"Sparkle Twins!" Brianna shouts, and I'm sure I see Naomi smirk. "Kylie and I love Luna and Lena," Brianna adds, making it so much worse. My little sister smiles up at me and I can't help what comes out of my mouth.

"I do not," I scoff. "It's for babies."

"But we—" Brianna starts but I cut her off.

"It's ridic," I say, and Brianna's mouth opens wide. "Enjoy your movie!" I tell my friends. "I hope it scares you to death." Then I march off toward theater 3.

Before we sit down in the velvet chairs you can lean way back in, my mother pulls my arm. "I know you're upset with your friends, but that's no excuse to take it out on your sister." I can hear she's not happy with me, but I can't help feeling annoyed.

And I'm so distracted that I can't even get caught up in Luna and Lena's adventure. I hardly care if Seebatch traps the twins in his dungeon of doors, because all I can see in my head is Naomi, Nikila, and Mara sitting next to each other in theater 4, sharing popcorn and screaming. And having fun without me.

About halfway through the movie, Momma gives me a pretty hard nudge—I guess I had sighed really loud or something—and so I try to pay attention, but it's like I'm the one who's gotten trapped and locked away behind one of Seebatch's monstrous doors.

I'm confused. If I had seen the movie with my friends, I would have been too scared to go outside when it rained. And because of my experiment, if my friends had said they were all going to the movie, I would've *had* to go too. So in a way, I should be thankful they didn't ask me. But how can I thank my friends for choosing to leave me out? I mean I'm already so worried about getting left out. That's *why* I'm doing the experiment. But I *don't* want to see Rain.

It's all so confusing and awful it makes me want to—

Oh no! I can't cry. This isn't fair. I sink lower in my seat and try to take deep, even breaths, which is what Momma always tells me to do when she sees I'm getting upset.

The breathing actually helps and after those first few tears, I'm able to pull myself together. I look over at Brianna and instead of watching the movie, she's watching me and I manage to give her a weak smile. She puts her small hand on top of mine and even though her fingers are sticky, I don't push her hand away.

When we get home, I put another check mark on my cry chart. I don't want to, but I can't pretend I didn't cry, and I can't fake like it was some physical pain like the shaving incident, when I know I had been sitting in a whole heap of hurt feelings. It still seems unfair because I wasn't doing what the whole group was doing and my experiment is based on that. And it was only a couple of tears. But I never quantified how many tears equaled crying, so now I have two check marks. (Quantifying is basically counting and you have to do it in science experiments.)

My first check mark was in red and my second one is in blue. I think I should have just used black. It seems silly to try to cheer up a sad little cry chart.

CRY CHART

☑ ☑ ☐

OBSERVATIONS

> When I saw the commercials for Rain, they freaked me out. I definitely did NOT (and still don't) want to see that movie. But friends shouldn't exclude other friends from stuff.
> My friends didn't seem to care that they were doing something without me.
> The whole point of my experiment is showing I'm as mature as my friends and that we should stick together. But what if they've already left me behind?
> Sometimes in books people will tell a

character they should have a good cry, like crying feels good. It doesn't.

Brianna knocks on my door, then pushes it open a little and pokes her head in.

"You're supposed to wait until I say 'Who is it?' before you open the door," I say in what Momma calls my Grumpy McGrump voice.

"Sorry," she says and closes the door. Then she knocks again.

"Who is it?" I ask.

She pushes the door all the way open this time and jumps in. "It's me!"

"Bree! You have to wait until I say you can come in," I say. We have gone over this before, but it's hard for a four-year-old to remember things.

She steps back out of my room and knocks for the third time.

"Who is it?" I ask again.

"You know it's me" is her muffled answer.

"Still," I say.

"It's Brianna," she says, her voice small and unsure.

Very formally, like I'm a queen and she is a fair maiden come to do my bidding, I say, "Oh, *please* do come in, Brianna."

She barges in and does a happy dance. Her wild dance erases my grumpy feelings. Sometimes a silly little sister can do that.

"I did it right!" she crows.

"Yes, you did," I tell her. "That's because you are super smart." I feel bad about how I acted. Momma was right. It's not Brianna's fault my friends left me out.

She giggles and then gets serious. "Do you want to do me a solid?" she asks.

"What is it?" I ask.

She walks over to my desk and touches the knob of the top drawer. Without turning around to look at me, she asks, "Will you play Lena and Luna with me?"

I figure after the movie, I owe her, so I say, "I can do that solid."

She whips around and has a huge smile for me. Then she walks over and sticks her hand out.

"Solid," she says.

"Solid," I say back, giving her hand a firm shake.

A little while later, the phone rings, and Momma says it's Mara. I say I'm too busy to come to the phone because Brianna and I are trapped in the bathroom trying to find the secret door that will get us out of the dungeon.

The phone rings again and this time Momma says I have to come to the phone because she is not a message service.

"Aha!" I say to Brianna. "My magic has returned, and I have unlocked Seebatch's evil dungeon."

"Yeah, Lena!" Brianna says, even though she always likes to be the one who saves us.

I open the bathroom door and head to the phone.

"Hi, Kylie," Nikila says.

"Hi," I say. "Why are you calling on the house phone?"

"You weren't answering my text messages."

I shoved my phone in my sock drawer when I got home so it isn't surprising I missed text messages. I was *trying* to miss text messages.

We listen to each other breathe for a few seconds and then she says, "You really wouldn't have liked that movie. It was so scary. I almost peed my pants."

If Nikila wants me to laugh at that she will get no satisfaction. She also isn't going to get me to say that she's right that I wouldn't have liked the movie.

By me not saying anything right away, Nikila must know I'm still upset, because she says, "But we should have invited you. I'm sorry we didn't." She pauses and then adds, "We're *all* really sorry."

"That's okay," I mumble even though it doesn't feel okay.

"We're going to get Froyo tomorrow, you wanna come?" Nikila asks.

How many plans did they make while the three of them were together? I wonder. But all I say is, "If everybody's going, then of course I'll go."

Good Thing

I love frozen yogurt. I love standing in front of the big silver machines, trying to decide whether I want to try plum or pomegranate or chocolate or tart. I love pulling down the handle and watching the frozen yogurt come out in a long, thick swirl like Rapunzel's hair, and I love fake panicking when it seems like you won't be able to shut off the machine in time. I love piling on fresh strawberries and mangoes, or sometimes granola.

When Mrs. Kumar picks me up, I climb in the back next to Mara and she gives me a little smile. I smile back because I don't want bad feelings between me and my friends. Naomi is on the other side of Mara, and she leans forward and smiles.

"Cute top," she says.

She has seen it a bunch of times, but I don't remind her of that. "Thanks," I say and swallow. "Yours is cute too."

Nikila is sitting in the front, and she changes the radio station from some slow music her mom was listening to, to 99.7. That's our favorite radio station. They play a lot of Queen Kitty. One of her songs comes on, and we all start singing along really loud. Nikila's voice is the best, so we let her take the lead part.

"You girls are ready for *America's Got Talent*! What voices," Mrs. Kumar jokes and we sing even louder.

Mrs. Kumar finds a parking spot, and after we all get out of the car, she says she's going into CVS to pick up a few things, so we can sit with our frozen yogurt at one of the tiny tables out front, and wait for her there.

Sitting with my best friends, eating delicious Froyo, I wish I had a way to erase that last check mark. It was silly of me to cry over not going to a movie I didn't even want to see.

When Naomi teases Nikila about how there's a storm brewing and she better watch out because it smells like rain, it doesn't even bother me. Not very much anyway.

Mara starts talking about a secret umbrella weapon she has tucked in her cloak and how she'll demolish the rain spirits.

Nikila shouts, "Don't go into the rain!" but of course she can't keep a straight face and starts cracking up.

I laugh along, but it actually does smell like it might rain, and a patter of goose bumps covers my arms. I am so glad I didn't go to that movie. I probably wouldn't be laughing now. "I can't believe you guys got to go to a PG-13 movie by yourselves," I say. As soon as I say it, I wish I hadn't, because it sounds sort of babyish and whiny. My friends pass around a look that seems like it belongs just to them and I don't like that. "What?" I ask.

Nikila puts a big scoop of frozen yogurt in her mouth and Mara clears her throat but doesn't say anything. Naomi shrugs. "What they don't know won't hurt them," she says, and licks frozen yogurt off her spoon.

"What's that supposed to mean?" I ask, but I have a bad feeling.

"We didn't *exactly* say we were going to see *Rain*," Naomi says.

"*What?*" I ask again in a loud voice.

"I did," Mara says, ignoring my question. She swirls her spoon around in her yogurt.

"Yeah, well, that's because you only had to ask Mady," Naomi says, sounding pouty.

I know that Naomi gets annoyed by Mara having fewer restrictions than the rest of us, but I still don't know what they are talking about. "I don't understand," I say. But then right away, I think I know. "You didn't get permission?"

Instead of answering me, Naomi says, "It wasn't even all that scary."

"So, you just . . ." I'm not sure I want to ask any more questions.

Naomi sighs like this is so preschool. "My mom and Nik's probably wouldn't have liked us going to see it. We just said we were seeing that movie, *Totally Random*." She raised her hands like, see, simple.

"You can't just tell your parents you're going to a different movie," I say. I know I sound bossy or like a mom-wannabe or something, but it makes me mad that they'd said they were seeing *Totally Random*, because we were supposed to all see it together. How are we going to see it now when *their* parents think they've already gone?

"What's the big deal?" Naomi asks. "It's not like we *really* lied. I told my mom I was going to the movies."

"Yeah, to see something else." I was leaning my chair back, but now I lean forward, crashing the front legs of the chair back on the ground. If I tricked Momma like that, I'd be in major serious trouble—because of course I'd get caught.

"Good thing we didn't ask you, then," Naomi says.

It's like she stomped on my toes. "Good thing," I say.

"Are you going to tell?" she asks.

I can't believe Naomi would ask me that. I don't answer because she should know I'm not going to tell on them.

"If you tell we'd all get in trouble," Naomi says. She is very serious, and her eyes are wide and worried.

"I wouldn't," Mara says.

"But I would," Nikila says softly and looks at me like she's really worried I just might tell.

"And I would too," Naomi says. "And I really can't—" She cuts herself off without finishing the sentence.

"No!" I say, hearing the sharpness in my voice. "I wouldn't do that."

Naomi settles low in her chair and eats a small spoonful of yogurt. "Okay," she says. She blinks rapidly, almost as if she is holding back tears but Naomi never cries.

I gnaw the edge of my spoon. I want to say they shouldn't do something like that again, and I want to say they shouldn't leave me out next time, but if they are going to be sneaking into movies I don't want to see and lying to their parents, then I'd rather they leave me out. I also want to say they should all know I wouldn't tell on them, even if I thought what they did was really wrong. I figure I'm better off just not saying anything and put a scoop of frozen yogurt in my mouth. Immediately, I get a horrible brain freeze. Even though it hurts, I'm almost glad because if I start crying I can pretend they are just tears from feeling pain.

That night a huge storm hits. The kind that only seems to happen in the middle of summer, with thunder and lightning and the windows rattling.

Normally, I love storms. But I keep thinking about those commercials for *Rain*, and it makes it hard to sleep.

Brianna comes into my room and I'm very happy to have company. I tell her how much I love storms, especially if there is lightning because it's magic. When I tell her this, her eyes open super wide, and she doesn't look scared anymore.

"Magic?" she whispers.

"Oh yes," I say. "The Sparkle Twins' world is right next to ours and sometimes it gets a little too close. And when *their* world bangs into *our* world, it makes a big booming sound and sometimes makes a crack. The boom is thunder, and the crack? That's lightning. If you look at it really close, Bree, you can see their world. That's why lightning's so bright because their world is super light and shiny."

"Really, Kylie?" Brianna asks.

I nod.

Right then we hear a huge crash of thunder, but instead of getting shaky and squirmy, Brianna claps her hands. After a few seconds, a streak of light fills the sky, and she runs to my window.

"I saw it! I saw it!" she says. "I saw their world. It *is* shiny!"

I have her climb into bed with me. "Let's wait for another peek," I say, and we sit side by side watching the window, hoping to catch a glimpse of the Sparkle Twins' world.

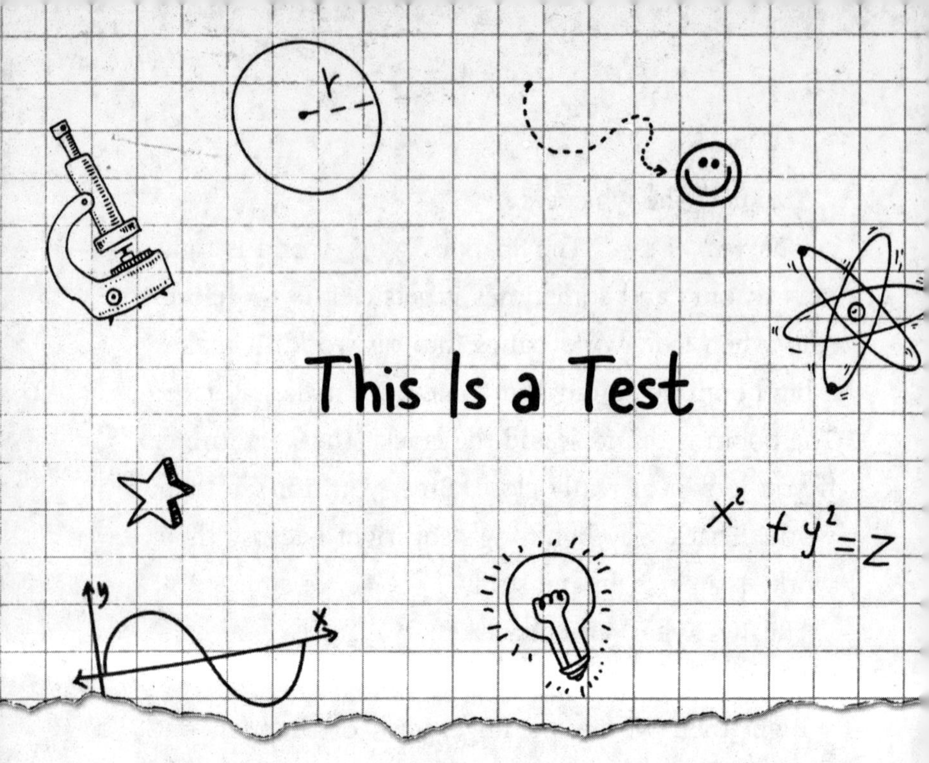

This Is a Test

In the morning, Momma says she has good news. "Dad will be home today."

Brianna and I both start shouting hurrahs.

He's been gone for such a long time, traveling to a bunch of different countries, selling software and training people there to be as good at selling software as he is. I hope if he trains enough people, it will mean he gets to be home more. Our family feels complete when he's here. I know it's a lot better for Momma when he's home, because then there's someone else who can shout at Brianna and me to settle down or make us eat our greens.

"He'll be excited to see what you've come up with for your kata," Momma says, and I gulp. She looks at me, and I know she suspects I haven't been working on it. "How's it going?"

"Uh . . . I have some ideas," I say.

Momma leans toward me. "Really?" she asks. "You want to show me some of it?"

It's obvious she knows that I have nothing. "I don't even get why I need to have an original routine. Just learning the regular stuff should be enough," I complain.

"The most wonderful scientific discoveries came from someone with a creative idea. A different way of looking at things." Momma smiles encouragingly. "I know you want to be a clever scientist. You'll need to exercise your creative bone."

"There is no such thing," I am quick to say but Momma has given me something to think about. I had never really thought about scientists being creative. The idea makes me smile.

"I have a humongous creative bone," Brianna says.

I grin at my sister. She is definitely more creative than I am. It's sort of nice that at least creativity doesn't seem to have much to do with being mature.

* * *

It seems like it takes forever before Momma finally says it is time to head to the airport. Brianna and I both start shouting "Yay! Yay!" and run to the car.

The High Street Bridge is up when we get to it and so we have to sit in a line of cars waiting to cross. This completely dampens our mood.

It may sound cool to live someplace where there are drawbridges you have to cross, like you live in a castle or something, and sometimes it *is* fun to pretend the bridges are magical, but mostly it is a pain. When the bridge is up you have to wait and wait for it to come back down so you can go across. Waiting for things is hard.

"I should've gone the other way," Momma mutters. She seems anxious and I know she is missing Dad as much as me.

She taps her fingers on the steering wheel and rolls down the window and takes a deep breath. Then she turns the radio down. "Are you still enjoying following behind your friends and doing what they do?" she asks me.

I can tell by the question that she's hoping I have some horrible stories about being forced to lick the bottom of shoes or something—as if everybody would want to do that! "My *science* experiment is going fine,"

I say to remind her that I'm not just trying to have fun. I wonder what Momma would say if I admit that I've already cried twice and have only one more cry left. Thinking about that worries me, but that's actually way down from my cry average. I'm sure I would've cried about *not* getting to go places and do stuff. I just wish that bad stuff wouldn't keep mixing in with the good things.

Momma glances at me a few times as if she is waiting for me to say more, but when I don't, she says, "That's good." She hums to the music playing on the radio for a moment but then says, "Sometimes, Kylie, your friends might want to do something you know is wrong and I would hope you wouldn't follow along."

Does she know about them seeing the movie without permission? I don't say anything in case this is a test. If she starts asking me questions, I know I'll have to tell her everything. It's not like I could get away with lying.

"I know your friends are good girls. I don't want you to think I'm saying they're not."

"I'm a good girl too!" Brianna calls out and I let out a little relieved sigh. I don't think Momma knows.

"You are very good, Bree," Momma says, smiling at her. Then she looks at me. "But even good girls make mistakes. And sometimes a friend could be going through hard times and sort of . . ." Momma pauses as she thinks of what she wants to say. "Act out," she finally says. "So, *think* about what the group wants to do, okay?"

"Okay," I say. I think about Naomi being mean sometimes. Is that acting out? I want to ask Momma, but that would be telling on Naomi and good friends don't do that.

The bridge finally comes down and Momma can start driving again and I listen to the bumpity-bump sound our tires make as we cross.

Just a little while later, Momma swings into the passenger-loading zone at the Oakland Airport and I look up and down the busy sidewalk, trying to find my dad.

"There he is!" I shout and jump out of the car. "Dad! Dad!"

Brianna is right behind me.

Dad opens his arms wide enough for both of us, and we plow into him.

After some hugging and giggling, he straightens up, but we keep clinging to him like baby possums. "Uh-oh, security is giving your mom the evil eye. We better head to the car," he says.

Brianna and I pile into the back but lean hard against our seat belts so we can be as close to Dad as possible. We start pestering him with questions before Momma has even had a chance to give him a hello kiss.

On the drive home, Brianna tells him how lightning is magic, and Dad sends me a wink through the rear-view mirror. If I knew how, I'd wink right back.

The bridge is down when we get to it, and we whisk right across without having to stop.

"The knight gallantly gallops across the bridge," Dad says. "He's been gone too long and he's anxious to return to his kingdom where he has heard tale of a speedy penguin."

"It's *zippy*, Daddy!" Brianna cries. "Not speedy."

Dad just laughs and I laugh too because he is very silly.

I hope he doesn't need to take another trip soon.

OBSERVATIONS

> I thought only artists were creative but scientists are too. This is good to know.

> Dad being gone + me having to be mature about it = A big achy pain in the middle of my chest.

Dragon Breath

A few days later, Dad says, if my friends want to, he'll take us all to Great America. Great America has lots of roller coasters and water rides and food and stuff.

"Can you just take us and drop us off?" I ask, knowing how happy Naomi and Mara would be if I could set up an unchaperoned day at a theme park, but my dad shakes his head.

"And miss out on the great rides and funnel cake? Why do you think I'm offering?" he asks.

I'm not sure if he's kidding, and I'm also not sure if my friends will want to go if my dad is going to be shadowing us around. He's a great dad, but he can be embarrassing. Screaming behind us on roller coasters, dancing on the runway stage, and spraying us with the water cannons—those are exactly the types of things he'd do.

Sometimes I think my dad can read my mind, because the next thing he says is that he will be hanging out at the little kid rides with Brianna and running through the water sprinklers, so my friends and I won't have the pleasure of his company. He says we can walk around by ourselves as long as we check in with him every once in a while.

I start clapping like a little kid, that's how excited I am.

"Are you sure, Rob?" Momma asks right away, trying to spoil the whole thing.

"Sure, I'm sure," Dad says and starts jumping up and down. "I'm dying to go!"

He is so ridic.

Luckily my friends don't seem to mind that my dad isn't just dropping us off. I think they are sort of impressed that he is letting us just run around the park unchaperoned.

The first ride Naomi wants to go on is Tiki Twirl. I

love that ride too, so I'm ready to race right to it, even though it means passing lots of other great rides.

"Why don't we ride the rockets first?" Mara asks. "We're right here."

Naomi gets a little pinch to her face. "We'll come back to them. The line gets so long at Tiki Twirl. Come on, let's go!" She starts walking away and Nikila follows her.

"Yeah, Mara," I say. "We'll just come back to these."

Mara crosses her arms and stares at me. "That doesn't make sense."

Naomi and Nikila have stopped and are looking back at us.

"Everybody wants to go on Tiki Twirl first," I say. I don't really care what ride we go on first, but since Naomi and Nikila have already decided to go there, it seems silly to argue.

"Ob-vi-ous-ly," Mara starts, stretching out the word like it's one of those super long snakes you can win at the game booths, "everybody does *not* want to start with Tiki Twirl because I want to start with the rockets."

I'm pretty sure Mara doesn't care what ride we get on first, she just doesn't want Naomi to get her way. Sometimes this happens with Mara. It's like she sees what Naomi wants to do and then picks the other thing. I think they both want to be the boss. I don't see why anybody has to be the boss.

By now, Brianna and my dad are probably already on their first ride. "Let's just decide," I say. All I want to do is get going.

Naomi takes a step toward us and that's enough for Mara, because she unfolds her arms. "We can start with Tiki Twirl, I guess," she says. "But I get to pick the next ride."

"Let's go!" Nikila says and we dash off together.

The thing that makes the Tiki Twirl ride great is that when you get strapped to your seat, and the big disk starts slowly rotating around, at first, it seems like no big deal. And then before you know it, the wind is blowing the skin on your face back while you hold on tight to the safety bar, and you're yelling because the disk is spinning fast and swinging way up high and you can pretend you're flying or falling off the earth.

When the ride stops, our legs are wobbly and we're all out of breath and we are grinning like we just aced the hardest test.

"Let's go again," Mara says. "But this time I'm going to put my glasses in my pocket. I almost lost them!"

I quickly look at Naomi because I'm sure she'll say

something to make Mara feel bad about choosing the same ride she did, but she just nods and says, "Yeah."

We go again and then we head to Psycho Mouse, which is my pick, then the swings, which is Nikila's.

When we get in line for the ride that's like going through wild rapids, we are behind four teenage girls. They all have their hair in sloppy buns. Their shorts are all tiny and they have bikini tops on under their T-shirts and they are wearing a lot of eye makeup. I don't understand why anyone would wear makeup to a theme park, especially if you're going to go on a ride where you are guaranteed to get a face full of water. These girls don't look like they are having fun at all. Why are they even here? They are all scowly, and they sigh a lot. I wonder what it is about being older that means you have to be so frowny.

We can hear them talking about some girl and calling her bad names.

"*Everybody* hates her," one of the girls says.

It would be awful to be the girl everybody hates. It makes me think of Melody. Does she think that everyone hates her? I wish I had been nicer to her. I wasn't *mean*, but I never even asked if she wanted to sit with all of us—the big group of girls that ate lunch together. Maybe not asking *is* being mean.

When we get off the ride, we are soaked. There are a couple of places as you are riding in your big round boat where people can shoot water rockets at you. And there are places where the ride stops and buckets of water rain down. Sometimes, only one person on the ride gets it, but this time, we all got splashed. I wonder if those teenage girls now have big black streaky lines running down their faces from all their makeup. It might not be nice, but I hope they do.

We slosh to the next ride, and then stop for garlic fries at the food mall. Once we grab a table, we dive into our fries and drink lemonade. I can't decide what I like more, the taste or the smell of garlic fries.

Naomi takes a sip of her drink. "I'll pass on the fries," she says. "Don't need to catch that dragon breath."

Before I can stop myself, I say, "Why? Cory's not here." Then I giggle like I'm hilarious, but inside, I'm thinking, *Uh-oh.*

"Seriously, Kylie, you're such a child," Naomi says.

"I am *not*," I say sounding way too much like Brianna.

"I still don't see why you can't just admit you kissed him," Mara says. "It's not like anyone cares."

"I care you don't believe me," Naomi says and her voice sounds tight and angry. "I said I didn't."

She doesn't look at me when she says this, and I wonder if it's because she and I both know she's lying and it's probably easier to lie to someone who doesn't know you're lying.

I think about what Momma said about acting out. But if Naomi is dealing with something she should tell us about it. Nothing seems to have changed except her.

She finally looks at me, but it's a mean look and I feel like she's just given me a push. I can feel tears gathering in my throat, but I swallow them away. Naomi is **not** going to make me fail my experiment.

"Moving on," Nikila says.

"Fine," I say and shove some fries in my mouth. The fries near the bottom of the container are so garlicky that my eyes water a little bit. But that's not crying.

"Fine with me too," Naomi says, like I was arguing.

I don't want to argue.

And then I decide something.

Friendship Oreo

I take a deep breath. "You know it was so hot and sunny that day. And I had salt water in my eyes. I just thought you guys kissed, but obviously you didn't." I say it really fast to get the bad-tasting words out of my mouth. It's sort of like buying a birthday present for your friend that is so cute that you really want it, but you have to give it to them anyway.

Naomi gives me a weird look that could mean she really likes the gift I just gave her, or that she doesn't think it's cute at all, or that she can't believe I pulled off a lie, but we all start talking about other stuff.

Before we leave the table, Melissa and Miriam—

M&M—come running up.

"Hi!" Melissa says.

My friends and I like doing everything together, but sometimes Melissa and Miriam take it too far. Like today, they are wearing matching outfits. Not sort of matching, like T-shirts and shorts, but the same purple sparkly T-shirt and the *same* faded blue capris.

Mara says, "Hey, M and M."

"We're having the best time!" Miriam says.

"Us too," I say.

"Have you seen anyone else?"

"Did your mom drop you off?

"Do you know when we get our schedule?"

"Those shoes are so cute, where did you get them?"

"Is it always just you four together?"

"Are you still going to jump rope at Douglas?"

M&M's questions are asked so fast there is barely time to answer, and I glance over at Naomi, and she nods knowingly and mouths "Spies," which makes me giggle.

"Have you gone on Drop Tower yet?" Melissa asks.

"No, we don't like that one," I quickly answer. I'm hoping this is still true. I know I don't like Drop Tower. The idea of being pulled up so high and staring down at the ground waiting for someone to let you fall isn't fun to me. And it has never seemed like fun to my friends either.

"Seriously?" Miriam asks. "*Everybody* loves it! It's the best!"

"Tiki Twirl's better," I say. "Hey, you guys, should we do Tiki Twirl again?"

"Let's try Drop Tower," Mara says. She glances over at me.

"Yeah," Naomi says.

When did this happen? Just last summer we all stared up at the legs we could see dangling from the Drop Tower seats and said we'd *never* ride it.

"It's so fun!" Melissa says.

"Fun?" I ask. "You must define that word differently than me."

"You're so silly, Kylie!" Miriam says.

"Let's go do Tiki Twirl," I say again. "We like that the best."

"Yeah," Nikila says. "Drop Tower is *wicked* scary."

I'm so glad someone is on my side, but before I can celebrate not going, Melissa says, "Chicken?" to Nikila and even has the nerve to *bwok* at her. Miriam starts flapping her elbows like wings. Considering we are just about seventh graders now, we should be too mature to do something just because someone calls us a chicken for not doing it, but Nikila turns to me and says, "Let's try it, Kylie."

Nikila, Naomi, Mara, and I form a friendship Oreo. Naomi and Mara are both a little more daring, and bold, and extroverted, so they are the crunchy hard outside part, and Nikila and I are both a little more careful. We're the soft middle. It's all delicious and works together. That's why our friendship is so great. Nikila switching to their side is hard for me. It makes us lopsided. I don't like it.

"Yeah, don't be a chicken," Melissa says to me.

Just because that worked on Nikila, doesn't mean it's going to work on me. "I don't want to," I say. But in my head, I'm thinking, *Oh no. Oh no! Oh no!!*

"Cut it out," Mara tells Melissa. "Kylie is as brave as anybody."

Although I really appreciate Mara sticking up for me, I still don't want to go on Drop Tower.

"Come on, Ky," Naomi says. "We're *all* going to go on. It'll be fun."

No, it won't. I wish I had never had the idea of doing everything my friends do. Right now, that seems like such a bad idea. But I'm not ready to call my experiment a failure over a ride. Even a ride that is scary and doesn't seem fun at *all*. "Fine," I say in a small voice.

Drop Tower is a big donut that is on a tall (really, really tall) tower. Once you get strapped in, the donut gets raised to the top of the tower, and then they drop you. The ride is also called Scream Zone because you can hear the riders screaming all across the park as they go down.

When we all get strapped into our seats, I suddenly have to use the bathroom. Really bad.

But before I can ask the attendant if I can get off so I can run to bathroom, there is a loud clicking noise and we start moving up. Nikila starts to scream, which is a little silly since we're not even at the scary part yet.

M&M are both giggling. I think they sound like howler monkeys.

When we reach the top, you can see the entire park. Somewhere down there, Brianna and my dad are running through sprinklers or watching the bubbles float around them on the little pirate ship. I wish I was with them. I wish I was not copying my friends. I wish I had not had so much lemonade. I wish I had been smart enough to say I would watch from the ground and just admit my experiment is a failure.

Naomi yells out, "Fee, fi, fo, fum!" which is actually sort of funny.

I guess this *is* what it would be like to be a giant.

And then my stomach is in my throat because we're rocketing down to the ground. I have almost a full second to think I'm going to pass out, and then we slow down and do a little bounce thing and then back up and down again. For a few minutes we are a yo-yo.

And then the ride goes all the way to the ground and stops. The safety bars release.

I unstrap from the ride and wipe my eyes. I am not crying. The ride is just so fast, it makes your eyes water.

My friends and I all hug like we have just survived being chased by Stormtroopers.

"Oh my gosh," I say. "That was so much *fun!*" I'm a tiny bit embarrassed to admit this, but it is too true not to say. I want to go again immediately. I don't even have to use the bathroom anymore.

"We told you," Melissa and Miriam both say at the same time.

I'm so glad I came up with my experiment. I could have lived my whole entire life without ever knowing Drop Tower is probably the best ride in the whole park.

For the rest of the day, M&M stick with us like glue. It's not terrible, but it's not the same as if it were just Naomi, Mara, Nikila, and me. They are very curious girls and they ask questions constantly. Maybe they have scientific minds. Or maybe they *are* spies.

I'm actually surprised that they are staying with us, since they usually just hang together. But it's fun to be part of a big group and take up most of the pathway as we run from one ride to another. Miriam smuggled in a big bag of sour gummy worms, and she's sharing them with us.

Before we leave, M&M want to stop at a booth where you can get T-shirts and hats and sweatshirts spray-painted with your name. "Let's all get shirts!" Miriam says.

I think having a T-shirt with Kylie spray-painted on the front will be excellent and I'm all ready to agree when Naomi says, "They aren't even cute. And did you see how much they cost? That's ridic."

I'm shocked because:

a) the shirts *are* really cute, and

b) I've never known Naomi to care how much something cost before. Mara is usually the one that thinks things are too expensive.

a + b = doesn't make any sense

"But if we all get them it'll be *so* great," Melissa says. "We'll all look alike. Wouldn't that be awesome?"

"Do you want to all wear our shirts on the first day of school?" Miriam asks like we have said we are all getting them.

As much as I wanted a shirt, dressing like M&M

on the first day does not seem like a great idea to me. It would make it seem like they were part of our group . . . or we were part of theirs. Hanging out with M&M has been fun but I don't want my group to be different.

M&M are not going to change Naomi's mind because her arms are folded across her chest, and she is frowning.

Mara checks out the price chart and says, "Even the key chains are too expensive!"

That settles it, and only M&M get shirts. I see the disappointed look on Nikila's face but it changes to a smile when Melissa says, "You're all invited to my birthday party."

"It's gonna be great!" Miriam says as if it is her party too.

I love birthday parties. I almost don't care what we do: bowling, ice-skating, watch a movie, play games at home. Whatever it is, it's all good to me. Eating cake and ice cream and seeing what cool stuff your friend got and what they put in the goody bag for you. I'm glad we ran into M&M because I'm not sure if Melissa really would have invited all of us to her party. Kids who have summer birthdays don't have to worry about hurt feelings since invitations aren't being passed out at school.

Last year, Melissa's party was at Super Jump, where they have tons of trampolines, and I didn't get invited. I had to hear how fun it was from Mara. I told Mara she only got invited because her name starts with an M, but really it's because Mara's mom and Melissa's parents go to the same church.

Naomi's frown has disappeared, and she gives Melissa a high five. "Excellent!" she says.

OBSERVATIONS

> Terrifying rides can be fun.
> Doing what everybody else does doesn't mean you have to dress exactly alike.
> Spray-painted name shirts are definitely cute.
> Maybe part of being mature is worrying about how much things cost.

Going Down

"Kylie, it's time to leave for karate school!" my mother shouts and even though I want to shout back that it's called a dojo, not a school, I don't shout anything because I'm not speaking to her.

She has totally reneged on our experiment deal.

My friends all went to the Santa Cruz Boardwalk and Momma wouldn't let me go. She said she was using the power of the veto, but I think she was using the power of the unfair mom.

She didn't even reflect on the problem or anything when I asked, and it's not as if I can complain to my dad and see if he would override her veto, because he left last night for Tokyo. He was home for only two weeks this time, and maybe the reason Momma is being so unreasonable is that she's just as sad as I am about him being gone again.

She didn't say that was the reason though. She gave me her list of reasons like they were part of one of her reports:

1. Mady is driving, and he is only seventeen.
2. Santa Cruz is over an hour drive away.
3. Mady is meeting up with "the fellas," so he will not be in charge of us, which means we'd be walking around the boardwalk by ourselves.
4. My mother does not like Mady.

Actually, she didn't say number four, but I'm pretty sure she was thinking it. She tried to say the whole plan was dangerous, so it couldn't be part of my experiment, but I don't see where the danger is.

Mady's been a fully licensed driver for over a year, and although he got into an accident last summer and banged up the front of his mom's car, he's gotten much better since then. Mara said he hardly ever gets speeding tickets anymore. And his car comes equipped with seat belts and airbags, so it would be totally safe. And as far as us walking around by ourselves, that's the whole point! We want to have fun on our own without having some parent lurking over us. Summer will be over soon, and we haven't crammed nearly enough grown-up, independent stuff into it.

It is strange that Nikila's parents let her go, because usually they're just as quick to say no to things as Momma. Then at least it's me and Nikila *together* not doing something fun. When it works out like that, Nikila and I groan with each other about how unfair our lives are, and how it is completely horrible to be us, and how lucky Mara and Naomi are that they get to do stuff all the time.

I was so mad when Momma told me that I couldn't go, that I talked back and used a "tone," and Momma took away my phone and said I could get it back when I learned to be respectful. If that was supposed to make me less angry with her, then her plan backfired.

I stare out the car window the whole way to karate and won't answer Brianna when she asks me like a million times what's wrong. Finally, Momma tells Brianna to just leave me alone, but I sure don't thank her for that.

When we get to the dojo, I'm glad to see Mr. Kim

has the sparring gear out.

When I'm a little upset or a whole *lot* upset, I love to spar because I can kick or punch somebody without getting in trouble. I can kick really high, so when I do a roundhouse, I can reach my opponent's head. Generally, people don't like getting kicked in the head. Even when they are wearing a padded helmet, and you have pads on your feet.

Today I feel like I could kick down a concrete wall, that's how upset I am. Knowing that Nikila's parents said yes when Momma said no makes me mad enough to try to punch Chantel, the girl I'm paired up to spar with, but I have to go easy on her because she is only an orange belt. I'm still at brown since I haven't come up with my own creative routine. But brown is way above orange.

You aren't even allowed to spar until you earn your orange belt, so Chantel has only just started learning.

We circle around each other, and I try to throw a few punches, but she stays just out of my reach. Since she's too far away, that means she can't reach me either, so neither of us can score any points. In sparring you want to get three points before your opponent does in order to win. Kicks to the head count for two points, so those are great to get.

Chantel circles to my left, bouncing on the balls of her feet like she's a boxer, and I circle right and look for an opening. I try to hit her with a ridge hand, but she just ducks it, so I try a backhand, but she ducks that too. I have to give her credit for good defense, but she'd be doing much better if she would just try to hit me. *I'd* be doing much better if she tried to hit me. Then I could hit her.

This is a problem only girls have. You should see the boys. They act like they are trying to kill each other no matter what belt level they're at. I'm going to ask Mr. Kim if I can spar with the boys if I ever move up to advanced brown.

All of a sudden, Chantel hauls off and kicks me in the head.

I'm so stunned, I stop moving, and she punches me in the chest! Mr. Kim is always telling me that I have a problem with my focus, and I guess he's right because I sure didn't see that coming.

"Oh my gosh! I'm sorry!" Chantel says, although it comes out sounding like, *Aw muh gwawrsh! Uhm shoreer,* because she has her mouth guard in.

Our judge, Sara Kosha, holds up three fingers showing Chantel won the match.

I take out my mouth guard. "Good job," I say, and

smile, even though I don't want to. She really shouldn't have hit me when my guard was down. Everybody knows that's a cheap shot, but I'd sound like a bad sport if I point that out.

"Are you okay?" she asks.

"Yeah," I say. It didn't really hurt anything but my feelings.

Mr. Kim shouts out for us to keep going, so I put my hands up. "That's one match for you," I say. I hope she knows I'm done messing around.

I start circling her, focused now. I can't believe I let her win. It's totally Momma's fault. I shouldn't even be here. I should be at the Santa Cruz Boardwalk, getting soaked on the water log ride and eating cotton candy. (Not at the same time of course.)

I want to give Chantel a sort of hard tap, so she'll know she's not dealing with some baby, but she's bending over and bouncing up, circling, and making it very hard to get her. I stop what I'm doing and drop my hands so I can explain she can't spar like that, and that's when she kicks me again!

"Oops," she says and giggles.

Okay, I think. It's time for her to go down.

I hit her in the side of the head with the edge of my left hand, spin around and kick her with a roundhouse, and then do a quick backhand. That's four points for me, so this time I win.

"Wow, you're really good," Chantel says.

"Sorry," I say. My face heats up with embarrassment. She is just a beginner. "I should've gone a little easier on you."

"That's okay," she says. "Besides, we both won a match."

I don't say anything because I still don't like her winning one match. But then Mr. Kim comes over and tells me I'm doing a good job working with a lower belt. He says I'm really showing maturity.

I don't want to tell him that he is congratulating me for not paying attention; I just bow my head a little. I sneak a glance over at Momma, but she isn't watching. She has created a little office with her laptop open and files on the chair next to her. She's probably deep into analyzing her dissertation topic, which is about different cultures having the same stories.

I'm disappointed she's not watching, because I would like her to hear at least someone thinks I'm being grown-up. I have to figure out how to tell her about this, without actually talking to her.

When class is over, instead of just watching Briana's class like I usually do, I go over to the practice corner so I can work on my original routine. I still don't have a single move.

After just standing there for a few minutes, I start kicking and ducking and chopping at the air. I feel a little ridiculous. It's like when Brianna and I are playing Sparkle Twins. I pause mid-chop. I could totally use that. I duck to miss Seebatch's sword and then I kick him several times right in the stomach. It feels great and I'm glad no one knows I'm pretending to battle the evil Seebatch. I notice Mr. Kim is watching me and he gives me a tiny smile and a nod, so I guess I'm on the right track.

Nothing Is Worse

On the way home, Momma's cell phone buzzes with a new text message, but she can't read it while she's driving. But then a few minutes later it buzzes again.

"Kylie," she says. "Check my phone and see who that is."

Although she didn't say please, I rifle through her purse, find her phone, and check the message. My eyes get wide. Both messages are from Mrs. Kumar:

The first one says:

Nikila isn't answering her phone, can you tell her to call me?

Then the next one is:

Maybe you didn't get message. Just need to tell Nikila she left her retainer. Not a big deal but I'd like her to use it. Can I bring it over?

I put Momma's phone back in her purse.

"Well?" she says.

I don't answer right away. Nikila got her braces off just a few months ago and she always forgets her retainer. Normally that is no big deal. Today it is.

I know the messages mean that Mrs. Kumar thinks Nikila is over at my house, which means Nikila must've lied to her mom about where she was going, which is totally unlike her. She does what her parents tell her. Always. But then I think about the movie. I'm guessing that Naomi is being a bad influence on her.

I don't know what to do. There is no way for me to lie to Momma. Not only would she be able to tell anyway, but also, she will see Mrs. Kumar's messages as soon as we get home. I could've deleted them, but Mrs. Kumar would've just texted again and then I'd *really* be in trouble.

"Uh," I say.

"Yes?" Momma asks.

Nothing is worse than having to tell your mother (who you're not even speaking to) something that you know is going to get one of your best friends in a lot of trouble.

"Mrs. Kumar wanted to know if she should bring Nikila's retainer over."

"Why would she want to know—" Momma stops in the middle of her sentence and looks quickly over at me before turning her eyes back to the road. She's gripping the steering wheel harder now. "Kylie," she says after a minute. "Why does Anu think Nikila is at our house?"

"I don't know," I say, which is completely not a lie.

"Can you *guess?*" Momma asks.

"Nikila probably told her that?" I say, making it sound like a question.

"Doesn't Anu know about Santa Cruz?"

It's possible that even though the plan was to go to Santa Cruz, my friends ended up somewhere else, so technically, I don't *know* Nikila's there and I also have no idea what her mom knows or doesn't know. I shrug. It seems unfair that Momma is grilling me because:

a) I haven't done anything wrong, and

b) after our fight this morning, she should be able to figure this whole thing out on her own.

a + b = leave me out of this

Momma must not understand this because she is

trying to put me right in the middle of the mess and asks, "Did Anu say Nikila could go to Santa Cruz?"

"I . . . I . . . uh, I don't know," I say, moving my mouth as little as possible.

"I should've known," Momma mutters. "It didn't sound like something Anu would let Nikila do."

I think Momma sounds a little too self-satisfied when she says that. I just bet she's trying to make me see that she's not the only unreasonable parent, but right now I'm not worried about that.

If Nikila had just listened to her mom and told Mara and Naomi she couldn't go, then I wouldn't have felt so bad earlier about not going, and Nikila and I could've hung out together and felt sorry for ourselves. And she sure shouldn't have told her mom she was going to be at my house like I'm an . . . accessory to her crime. (Me and my dad like watching crime shows together.)

When we get home, I go upstairs to my room and leave the door open. I want to hear how Momma's call goes with Mrs. Kumar. I can't tell much. I hear a bunch of "mm-hmms," and "they sure ares," and "I knows."

Brianna comes into my room, and she must know what I'm doing, because she is very quiet. She sits on my bed and kicks her feet and bounces a little.

When Momma hangs up, I wonder if I should call Nikila to tell her she is busted. Since I don't have my cell phone, I can't text her. I'd have to call her using the house phone. And if I do that, Momma might hear.

"Is Nikila in trouble?" Brianna asks in a soft whisper.

I nod.

"Because she did something wrong?"

I nod again.

"I did something wrong today," Brianna says, and stops bouncing.

I'm sure it's nothing awful, but she looks scared. "What did you do?"

"I used Momma's shaver," she whispers, and puts her arms behind her back.

"Let me see," I say.

She thinks about it, and then after a second, she holds out her right arm and I see a small hairless patch just above her wrist. It's hard to notice because Brianna doesn't have a lot of hair on her arms anyway. "Bree, you could've cut yourself," I say. "You're too little to use a razor." I don't say she is in big trouble.

"I wanted to be grown-up like you," she says and folds her arms so the shaved bit doesn't show. "But I didn't like it."

It's hard to tell your little sister that she is wrong for wanting to be like you. "You have to promise you won't touch those razors again, okay?"

"Are you going to tell on me?"

Momma always tells Brianna and me that she doesn't want us to be tattletales, but I think she'd want to know about this. Maybe because of what happened with her when she was young and shaved when Big Mama didn't know, Momma might be understanding instead of mad. But I'm sure Momma wouldn't appreciate me telling Brianna about when Momma broke the rules too, so I just say, "I'm not going to tell." Brianna smiles at me, but before she gets too happy, I add, "But I'm not going to *not* tell either." She frowns. "So, if she *asks* me, I'll have to tell her the truth. And so will you. Okay?"

"If you did something you weren't supposed to, would you tell on yourself?"

I should say yes. My parents always say I'm supposed to set a good example for Brianna, so I mean to say yes, but what comes out is, "I would . . . try to." I guess I can't even lie to Brianna. "And you know, Bree, she's probably going to notice."

Brianna stares down at her arm and she doesn't look at me when she says, "If she asks me, I'll tell her. Okay?"

And even though she hasn't asked me to do her a favor, I say, "Solid."

OBSERVATIONS

My pen *tap tap taps* on the paper. I didn't actually observe much except Nikila getting busted. Finally, I write:

- I would rather have my parents tell me no than sneak to do something and get caught. I'm really glad that Momma is letting me do the experiment even though I was very angry with her this morning.

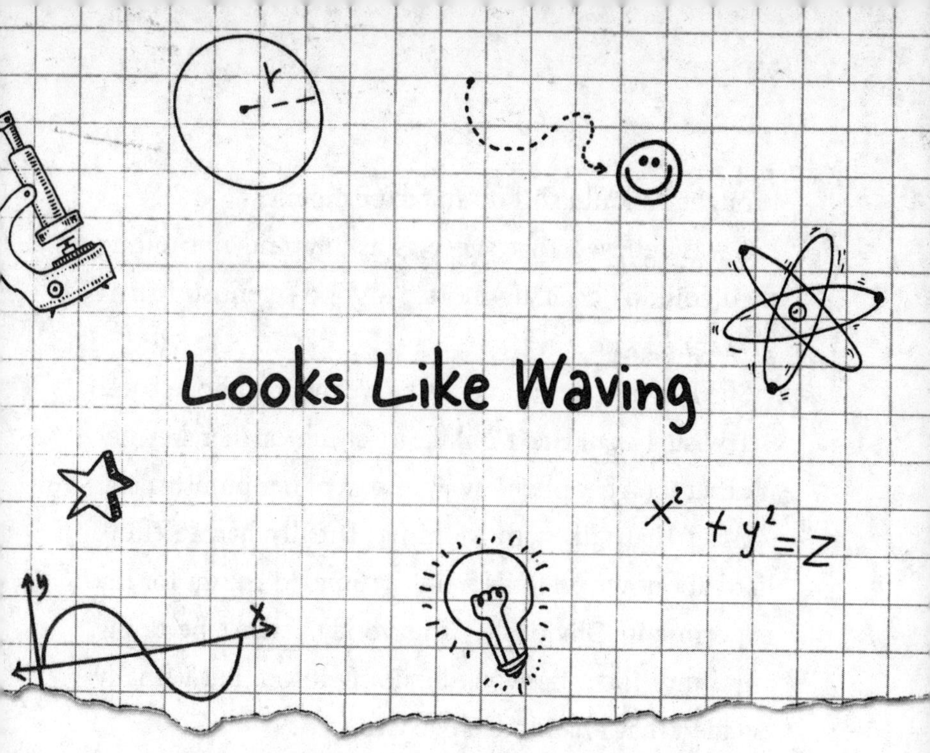

Looks Like Waving

Nikila is grounded for the rest of the summer, which means she can't go to Melissa's party. Naomi and Mara didn't get in trouble because their parents knew they had gone to Santa Cruz.

This seems unfair. I know Naomi was the one who convinced Nikila to lie, so it seems as if Naomi should get at least a tiny bit of blame. But Naomi never gets in trouble. Mara doesn't really either, except sometimes Mady is mean to her, and maybe that feels like trouble to her.

Momma had a long talk with me as if I had done something wrong. Then she asked me whether I thought I should still do my experiment.

I was relieved that she was asking and not telling me I couldn't do it anymore. "A good scientist doesn't give up," I said.

She laughed at that and also gave me my phone back.

I wish I could text Nikila to check on her but her mother took her phone away as part of her punishment.

After that talk with Momma, I really had to think hard about what Nikila being grounded meant for my experiment. Obviously, "everybody" won't be doing anything since she won't be doing it too. But I finally decided that I had to change Group A.

*Group A:
Naomi
Mara
~~Nikila~~
Kylie
* Due to unforeseen circumstances, Group A was amended.

It was awful crossing off Nikila's name because it felt like I was saying we weren't friends anymore, but really, I'm just removing her from the experiment. Still, it is yucky.

And it is still yucky a few days later when Momma drops me and Mara off at Naomi's, so Naomi, Mara, and I can all go to Melissa's birthday together. I wonder if my friends felt this bad when it was just the three of them going to the movies.

"Have fun," Momma says before we get out the car. "Make good choices."

"We will," Mara and I both say even though I want to say it isn't always so obvious whether a choice is a good one or a bad one.

When Naomi lets us in, I notice a bunch of boxes in the family room.

"What's going on?" I ask. My throat gets tight, and my shoulders suddenly feel heavy. "You're not moving, are you?"

"They're just boxes!" Naomi says all shouty, which clearly means they are more than just boxes.

Audrey says, "Nooms!" Usually when Audrey calls Naomi by her nickname, she uses a very sweet loving voice, but now she sounds exasperated. Like when Brianna has asked Momma to play Zippy the Penguin for the one hundredth time.

"Mom!" Naomi says back and she sounds annoyed too but her mom just flaps her hand as if she is saying, continue on your business.

Mara and I raise our eyebrows at each other, in that way friends do when another friend is being all weird. I mouth "Nik" to Mara because I am guessing that is why Naomi is in a grumpy mood. Maybe she is worried that it's her fault that Nikila isn't with us.

"It's not time to take you girls to the party yet," Audrey says. "And I know y'all don't want to help with this mess." She points at the boxes and Naomi shakes her head hard. "I know," Audrey says and rolls her eyes. "How about ice cream sandwiches outside?"

All three of us nod happily and we follow her to the kitchen. Once we have our ice cream, we go outside to sit on their deck.

"Stay under the umbrella," Audrey tells us. "You don't want to get too much sun." Then she goes back inside.

As soon as her mom is gone, Naomi moves her chair right out into the middle of the deck. She closes her eyes and leans back like she's on vacation.

It's really hot, and a bothersome fly has taken an interest in my ice cream sandwich and keeps landing on my hand, so I have to keep waving my hand around to keep the fly off me. I look like someone who keeps seeing a bunch of their friends every five seconds and has to wave at each one.

"I wish Nikila was here," I say and wave.

"Yeah," Mara says. "Her parents are so strict."

"For *real*," Naomi says. "I don't know how she stands it." She opens her eyes and takes a bite of her sandwich.

I wave. I can't really think of anything to say because it's nice out on the deck and I don't want to start an argument. I don't think Nikila's parents are all that strict; at least, they aren't any stricter than mine. I wave again. "Was it fun?"

Naomi and Mara look at each other like they have a secret.

"What?" I wave both hands now and almost lose my ice cream sandwich.

"It would've been more fun if Nikila hadn't complained every five seconds about being there," Naomi finally says.

Mara shrugs. "It was fine."

I'm not sure if that means she's agreeing with Naomi or not. "She probably knew she was going to get in trouble," I say. "It's hard to have fun when you're worried." When my friends told me they were going to Santa Cruz, I didn't think of just lying to Momma so I could go. Not because I'm so wonderful but:

a) I sure wouldn't have had fun knowing I was going

to get in trouble, and

b) as previously stated, I can't lie.

a + b = the plan wouldn't have worked anyway

Maybe Momma was thinking about stuff like this when she was warning me about my experiment.

Naomi stands up. "Let's go," she says, and I wish she sounded happier about going to a party.

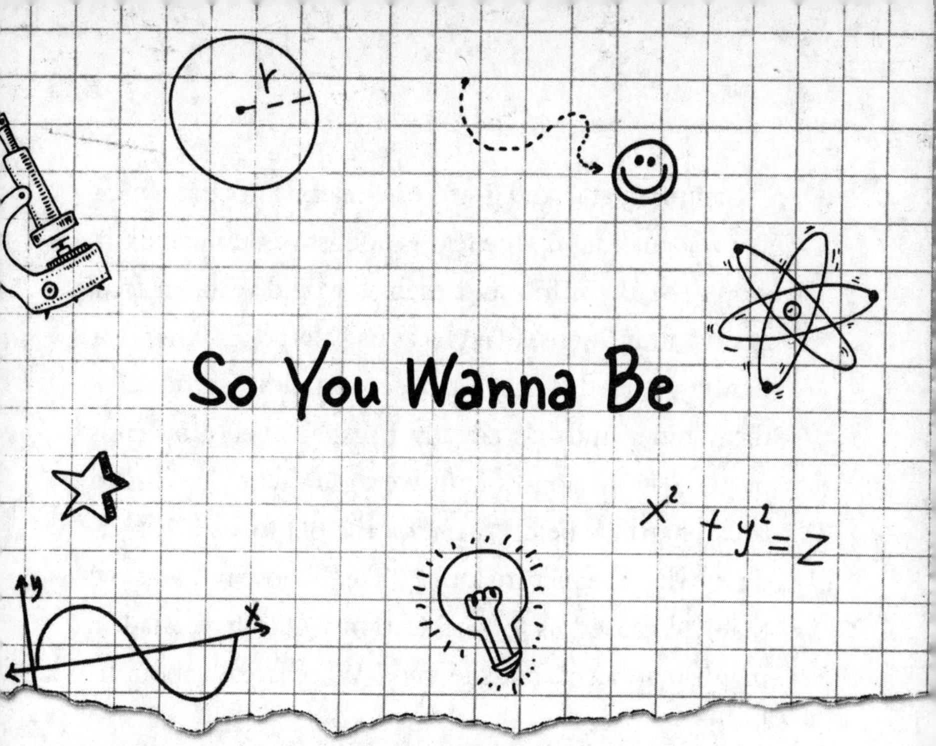

So You Wanna Be

Melissa's party is at Stoneridge Shopping Center. It's a fancy indoors mall, not like Shoreline at all. After we get dropped off at her house, her mom, Mrs. Nelson, loads all us girls into her oversized van. When we get to Stoneridge, she breaks us up into two teams (of course M&M are on the same team) and gives us a list for a scavenger hunt. It has things on the list like get a bag from the Gap, buy cinnamon pretzels, take a photo in the picture booth, listen to a sales pitch by one of the kiosk vendors, and stuff like that. Once we've checked off everything, we have to race back to the food court.

Naomi, Mara, and I are one team. I'm sure when she was making up the teams, Melissa assumed Nikila would be there too and then it would've been four against four. Melissa laughs at us slowpokes when we finally get to the juice place for samples. Her team is the winner and has already finished their tiny cups of juice. It is Naomi's fault we didn't win. She had to brush her hair before we took the photo, as if it mattered what the picture looked like. I know if it was me that had caused us to lose, Naomi would have made a big deal about it, but she says "Who cares?" about us losing.

Melissa says it's time for the best part of the party and leads us to So You Wanna Be.

I have always wanted a So You Wanna Be party. I've watched the girls who work there do fun hairstyles for all the party guests and do their makeup. Momma says it's a waste of money because I could just have a dress-up party at home, but obviously it's not the same.

All seven of us start squealing when we get into the store because the stuff in there is so cute. They have fuzzy pillows, and glittery cell phone cases, and bubble bath that smells like frosting, and lamps with sequins, and hamburger-shaped erasers.

Our party helper, Jamie, gives us a style sheet of looks and tells us we just need to pick the one we want. We can be rock stars, or princesses, or mermaids, or glamour girls, or movie stars. You get one free accessory with whatever look you choose, and I have my eye on the headband the mermaid wears. It has a string of tiny seashells along the whole thing, and each shell is absolutely perfect. I also like the way the mermaid has her hair done in big, fat curls and, of course, pushed back with that beautiful headband.

"We can pick any of these?" I ask, just to make sure.

"Yeah," Melissa says. "Don't you love the wireless microphone for the rock star?"

I don't love it. It's plastic and obviously doesn't actually do anything. It sits on your head sort of like a headband—but not a cute one—and has a mouthpiece that you can sing into. But what good is a microphone that doesn't *do* anything?

Before I can say I'm choosing the mermaid, Melissa says, "Let's all be the same thing! It'll look better for the picture."

Being the same would be fun, so I say, "Yeah, let's all do the mermaid, then we can all get the seashell headband. We could wear them to school!" I try to make my voice super excited. I hope you don't need to be a brainiac to realize you couldn't wear the microphone to school—unless you wanted to look like a dork.

"But if we're all rock stars, we'll look like we're in a band together," Miriam says.

I examine the hairstyle for the rock star. It's lots of twisted sections of hair, with the ends of each twist poking out. The girl in the picture has stick-straight hair, and the style looks good on her. It won't look good on me. My hair will look like a mess all twisted up that way. None of the other girls at the party have hair like mine. Last year for Christmas I asked Momma for a hair straightener, and she laughed. "Some people, Ky," she had said, "aren't meant to have straight hair." And obviously, she meant I was some people. And it meant I wasn't getting a straightener.

I don't hate my hair or anything, I just thought it would be nice to have hair like my friends for once, but now, standing there in So You Wanna Be, looking at the big curls of the mermaid and comparing it to the tiny twists of the rock star, I don't want to look like my friends if they all want to be rock stars.

"The mermaid is for little girls," Naomi says.

That is just plain ridiculous. I could understand if I was saying I wanted to be the princess. Even I know it's like at the school Halloween parade, where only the little girls dress up as princesses. By fourth grade you have to wear something scary (but still cute), or from a movie or TV show. Everybody knows that. Mermaids are fine. "That headband would look really pretty on you, Naomi," I try.

Naomi looks back at the style sheet. Then she looks at the display of headbands.

Mara asks Melissa, "Do we all *have* to pick the same thing?"

Before Melissa can answer—and I can tell by the way she and Miriam exchange looks what her answer is going to be—Mrs. Nelson says, "Of course not. You girls just tell the lady what you *wanna* be"—she winks at Jamie like they have a secret joke together—"and they'll fix your hair and then you get to put on the outfit that matches your look. And they'll take a group picture after." She gives Melissa one of those mother looks that means they must have talked about this before, in private.

I don't feel exactly relieved. If *everybody* wants to be a rock star then I'm going to have to be one too.

"The headband is pretty, but the rock star looks so cool," Mara says. "Nikila would love it."

Mara is right that Nikila would like to pretend to be

a rock star, but I am not Nikila.

Melissa claps her hands together like something was decided. "Let's all be rock stars!"

When Miriam nods, and Mara shrugs and the other girls start squealing, my mouth gets dry, and I get a pinch right between my eyebrows.

"Everybody's going to be a rock star," Melissa tells Jamie and Jamie smiles and nods.

"Line up girls," Jamie says. "Birthday girl first."

There's a velvet chair in front of a mirror with lights all around it, and when Jamie starts doing Melissa's hair, it looks like she's working on a celebrity.

Normally, I would fight to be next in line, or next after next, but today, I'm fine being last. I stand there and reflect on the problem as I watch Melissa's hair get twisted and held in place with a bazillion bobby pins. Then Melissa gets her makeup done. It's a lot of wild colored streaks and looks silly. The makeup for the mermaid is shiny body glitter that makes it look like you just got out of the water, and pale green-and-blue eye shadow. It's so pretty, and I bet those eye shadows would go perfect with my skin color.

Every good scientist knows that as you're doing an experiment, you need to pay attention to the results as you go along. You don't just wait until your experiment is over, because you might miss some important evidence. I haven't been a very good scientist because even though I have a bunch of observations, I haven't started analyzing any of my data. Like I should be working to figure out what it means that sometimes doing what everybody else is doing can be a whole lot of fun but sometimes what everybody wants to do is the exact opposite of what you want to do, and having to do it anyway is . . . sort of horrible. And what does any of it have to do with maturity? I promise myself that when I get home I'll go back through my observations and act more like the scientist I'm supposed to be.

I wonder what the hairstyle option would be for a scientist. I think of Albert Einstein and wish I could joke about that with one of my friends, but I'm sure no one else would think it was funny.

Naomi is ahead of me in line, and I notice she is holding a seashell headband. Probably if I had just talked a little faster, I could've convinced her that being a mermaid would've been way better than being a rock star. She's smart enough to know a headband you can wear in your actual, everyday life is better than a fakey microphone that will probably break before you even get it home.

The way Naomi is holding that headband—like it belongs to her—I'm sure she's already changed her mind, but when the helper asks "Who you wanna be, hon?" Naomi says, "Rock star." My stomach starts to hurt. It would have been so nice if she had said mermaid.

I feel weird getting my hair done with everyone standing around waiting. I avoid looking in the mirror in case I have made a mistake. I hear someone giggle when the lady is putting on my makeup and even though I tell myself they probably aren't laughing at me, I can't make myself believe it. I can't help but think about my experiment and that makes me want to cry. This whole maturity thing is really hard.

Once I'm done, we go to the dressing room to get into our outfits. We don't get to keep the outfits; it's just for the picture.

Where we change our clothes is just one big room, and we all have to get down to our underwear. At slumber parties, when it is time to get into pj's, we all take turns changing in the bathroom. I know at middle school, I will have to change in front of other girls for PE, but I haven't prepared myself yet.

Mara faces the wall to change. Naomi doesn't, but she takes her sweatshirt and jeans off very slowly like she doesn't want her clothes to get messed up. Then she puts on her rock star clothes. I'm a little surprised to see that all the other girls are wearing bras whether they need them or not. M&M must change in front of each other all the time because they are just giggling and telling each other how cute their underwear is.

I turn away from the rest of the girls to change my top. I'm going to tell Momma I need to start wearing a bra. It'll be a layer between me and the world.

One of the girls working in the store gets us lined up for a photo and Melissa directs where she wants everyone to stand. I am nowhere near Naomi and Mara. After we pose for our picture, we change back into our regular clothes, but of course we all leave our hair styled and our makeup on.

Mrs. Nelson says it's time for pizza in the food court. I wonder if the other girls will be embarrassed to walk around the mall in all that makeup. They don't *seem* embarrassed. They are acting like they are actually rock stars and pretending their microphones work. I don't act like a rock star. I'm over this party.

As we're leaving the store, Jamie stops Naomi. "Hey," she says. Jamie has been very nice and smiley with us all afternoon, but she isn't smiling now.

Naomi stares up at her for a second, then she starts biting the inside of her cheek.

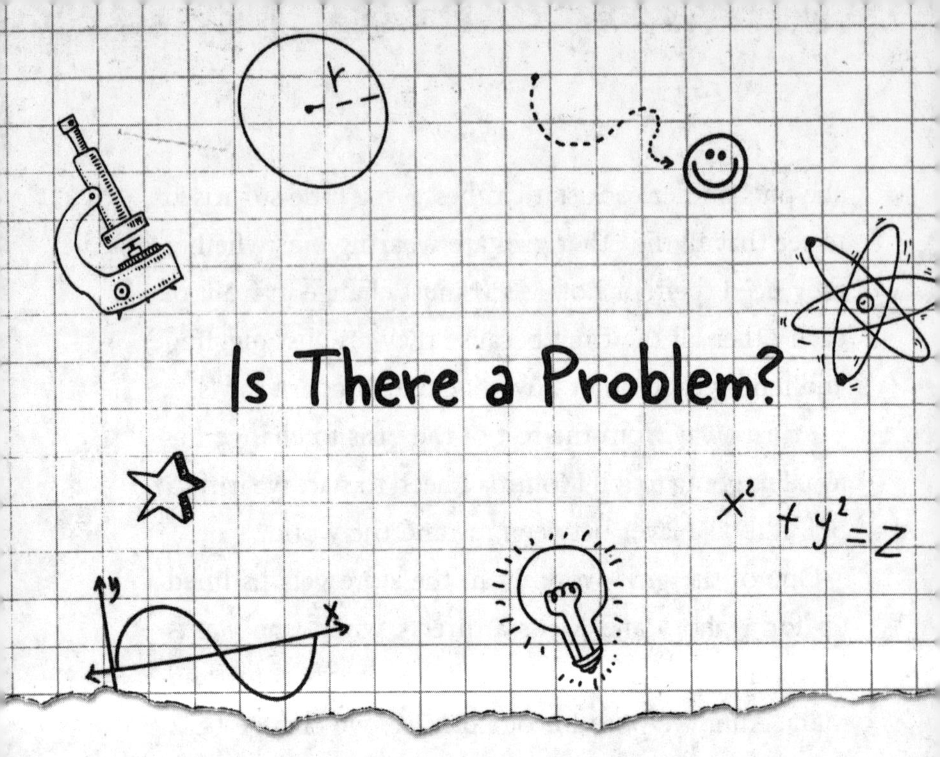

“The seashell headband is just for mermaids,” Jamie says.

I don’t know what is going on. Naomi has the microphone on her head, not the seashells.

Jamie holds out one of her hands, and she sets her other hand on Naomi’s shoulder. Jamie’s fingers look hard. “I *saw* you,” she says.

Mrs. Nelson turns around and asks, “Is there a problem?”

I know she is anxious to get to the pizza and have the party be over. Moms always look like this toward the end of birthday parties. Like they’re wishing they never had the idea in the first place, and then as you leave, they find their smiley face again, and tell you it was so nice having you, and hopefully hand you a goody bag. Mrs. Nelson's smile looks frozen, like someone is taking too long to take her picture.

Right now, it's like we are *all* frozen, waiting for whatever is happening between Naomi and Jamie to be over. Then Naomi reaches into the big pocket of her sweatshirt and pulls out a seashell headband. She holds it out to Jamie, but Jamie doesn't take it, and she doesn't let go of Naomi's shoulder.

I want to think that Naomi just made a mistake. That while she was getting her rock star outfit together, she needed to put down the mermaid headband and stuck it in her pocket, planning to put it back on the rack when we came out of the dressing room. That's what I want to think, but Naomi's face has gotten red, and she looks so scared, it's hard for me to convince myself. I think about rhinestone sunglasses. And I think about how Naomi has been lying all summer.

Jamie is holding her so tight that I can tell *she* doesn't think Naomi just made a mistake. Then Naomi does something she never does. She starts crying.

Like *tsunami* tears.

Maybe if you don't usually cry, when you finally

do, it's like all the tears you ever could've cried come out together. Something like that must be happening, because I have never seen so many tears.

Mrs. Nelson's face is all pinched up like she has bitten into the sourest pickle. She marches over and snatches the headband from Naomi. "You got the *microphone,*" she hisses at Naomi. Then she turns to Jamie. "I'm sure it was a simple misunderstanding," she says. I know she is trying to make sure Melissa's party isn't ruined. "Here's the headband, okay?" She sets the headband on the rack with all the other ones, and then wipes her hands on her pants.

"We'll need to talk to the manager," Jamie says.

"Oh, surely—" Mrs. Nelson starts, but she doesn't finish. She nods and then she says to us, "You girls wait here."

Jamie, Mrs. Nelson, and Naomi go through a door in the back of the store. Naomi is still crying, and her rock star makeup is ruined.

"Is she going to get arrested?" Denise Alba asks.

Melissa starts crying, but I don't know if she's crying because this is such an awful thing to happen at her party, or if she's worried about Naomi. Then Miriam starts crying and then *everybody's* crying. Everybody except me.

I cross my arms and stare at a sparkly fuzzy purple pillow. I wonder if the sparkles would make the pillow itchy. I wonder what is going on behind that closed door.

All the girls seem to be crying harder. Even Mara is crying, and she comes and stands next to me, so of course I have to uncross my arms and put one around her shoulder.

"What's going to happen to her?" Mara chokes out.

"I don't know," I say. The longer Naomi is gone, the madder I'm getting. I can't believe she took that headband.

"Don't you care?" Mara asks.

I do care. I guess I should be crying like everyone else. I wipe my eyes really hard, as if I had tears coming out. I pinch my nose, like it was about to start running. It seems completely unfair that I have cried so many tears in my life when I really didn't want to, when now, when I just want a few lousy tears to come out, just to show I care about Naomi too, I can't squeeze out a single drop.

No Excuse

I turn my mouth down in a big droop, but it's like my eyes are broken.

It seems like Naomi has been gone for a long time. Like a really long time. And I still can't help but be mad at her. Why couldn't she have just said she wanted to be a mermaid? She would've gotten the headband. Did she just say she wanted to be a rock star because everyone else was saying they wanted to do that? Suddenly, my experiment seems like a lousy idea.

When the manager comes out of the office, Naomi and Mrs. Nelson are right behind her. We all leave the store, but as we go, the manager tells Naomi she can't come back. When I hear that, I look at Naomi and she seems smaller than Brianna. It's as if she had been a balloon and someone stuck a pin in her.

Maybe it was having a large group of loud crying girls in the middle of her store that made the manager decide not to call the police. She just wanted us to get out of there.

As we leave the store, Mrs. Nelson chirps, "The pizza here is so dry. We'll have yummy snacks at home." She says it almost as if it had been her plan all along, but Melissa gets a big frown. She doesn't argue, though, and I'm sure it's because none of us are in much of a party mood anymore.

Back at Melissa's, Mrs. Nelson puts out some chips and cheese sticks and juice boxes and turns on a movie. Melissa's face is so stormy, I'm surprised her eyes don't shoot lightening at us.

Naomi goes and sits by herself in a corner and when Mara goes over to try to talk to her, Naomi just buries her face in her hands.

Audrey is picking us up, and when she gets to the house, Mrs. Nelson has a private talk with her, and then Audrey barks at us to get into the car.

For the first few minutes, as we drive along, no one says anything. Naomi stares out the window, Mara starts taking bobby pins out of her hair, and I tie and retie the woven belt I'm wearing. The radio is playing country music, and I know if Naomi was feeling better, she'd change it to 99.7.

I shouldn't have told Naomi the headband would look pretty on her. That must be why she tried to take it.

Audrey snaps off the radio. "You think your father moving out is an excuse for you to steal?" she asks.

Naomi doesn't answer.

I remember all the boxes at their house. Mr. De La Cruz is moving?

"Don't you think this is hard on me too?"

When Naomi still doesn't answer, Audrey slaps the steering wheel hard, making me jump.

"Well?" she asks, as she cuts off a car next to us. The driver of the other car honks, but Audrey ignores him.

"Are you trying to kill us?" Naomi asks.

Now Audrey doesn't answer Naomi.

It gets quiet in the car again, and then Naomi says, "You don't seem like you even care."

"About you stealing? You bet I care about that!" Audrey snaps.

"About Dad," Naomi says, and her voice is low and solemn. Very un-Naomi.

Audrey glances in the rearview mirror at Mara and me, and then she goes back to watching the road. "We'll talk about it later," she says.

I get dropped off first and Audrey waits until Momma opens the door before she drives off.

"Wow, look at you," Momma says.

I do what I always do when Momma says that. I do this weird thing with my eyes, as if I'm actually trying to see myself. I know it makes me look odd, but I can't help it, it's a habit.

Then I tell her what happened. About Naomi stealing. I still can't believe it. "I shouldn't have told her she would look great as a mermaid," I say.

"Come sit down with me, Kylie," Momma says, and I follow her to the sofa.

I slump down like a limp noodle.

"You didn't do a single thing wrong," Momma tells me. "And I'm sure you were scared in the store. Even when something isn't happening to you, it can feel pretty awful."

I nod fast. "I was really mad too," I admit.

Momma gives me a small understanding smile. "Mad. Hurt. Disappointed. Sad. Confused. Maybe even relief that it wasn't happening to you. A whole bunch of feelings swirling around."

"Yeah," I say.

"All of those emotions are normal so don't worry about that. And I know things are hard for Naomi right now. But that's no excuse for her to steal," Momma says.

"You knew Mr. De La Cruz was moving out?" I ask Momma, but realize before she even says yes that of course, Audrey would have told her. That's why Momma had that talk to me about people acting out when they are going through hard times. But things are hard for me too. "I miss *my* dad, but I don't steal things." My bottom lip pokes out, which I know makes me look like a baby, so I try to pull it back in, but it doesn't want to go.

"Naomi taking that headband? That was very wrong, no matter what she might be going through." Momma puts her hand on my shoulder. "But sometimes we have to be more understanding than we're ready to be. You can hate the crime without hating the criminal, okay?"

Momma's hand is soft and comforting and not at all like Jamie's looked like when she was gripping Naomi. I wonder if Momma realizes she just called Naomi a criminal.

"But if she wanted a seashell headband, all she had to do was be a mermaid," I say. It seems so simple to me.

"What did she dress up as?"

"A rock star. *All* the girls were rock stars." I see Momma raise her eyebrows and I know what she is thinking.

"I *know*," I say. "My experiment is just a big flop." And suddenly the tears that I wanted to come just a little while ago show up unannounced and unwanted and I can't stop the river dribbling down my face.

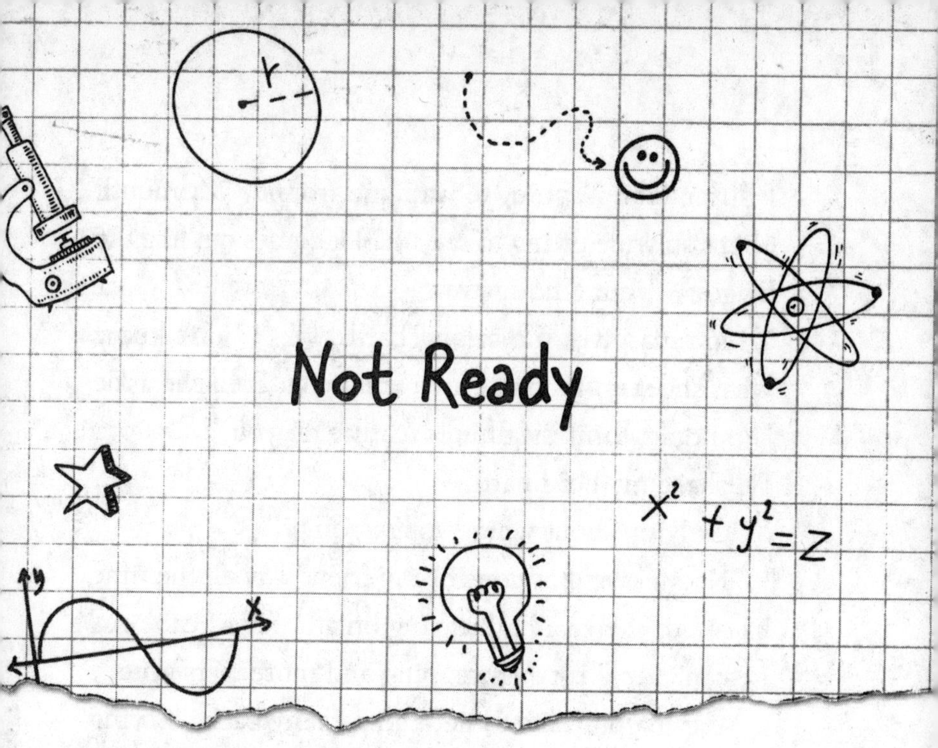

Not Ready

"Kylie, what's wrong?" Momma asks, but I just cry harder. "Did something else happen?"

When I don't answer, she pulls me into a close hug and just holds me like that until my sobs slow down.

"Is there something wrong with me?" I ask in a shaky voice.

Momma releases me from her tight hug and stares at me in confusion. "Kylie, what in the world are you talking about?" she asks.

"I don't know h-h-how . . ." I stammer, trying to talk through my tears. "To be m-mature," I finally say. "Maybe I'm not ready for seventh grade and my f-f-friends aren't going to want me around." My mouth opens so wide trying to say *around* it comes out like the biggest whining noise ever.

Momma gives me a long hard look. I don't know what she sees. Probably a big baby. But then she asks, "You don't think stealing is mature do you?"

I shake my head hard.

"Or lying about where you're going?"

"No," I say. "But none of my friends *cry* all the time like I do." I take a big heaving breath. "But I can't . . . I c-can't . . . " I start hiccuping and more tears erupt.

Momma pulls me to her and pats my back. "Crying is just an emotional response." She gives me a little squeeze then pushes me away so she can look me in the face. "Think of how wonderful you are with your sister. *That's* showing maturity."

"But . . ." Playing with Brianna seems like the opposite of being mature. I wipe my face. "My experiment was supposed to prove I was mature by not crying. To show I was the same as Mara and Naomi and Nikila. I'm younger than them and they've been acting like . . . that's a problem." Saying it out loud puts me right on the edge of bursting into tears again.

Momma looks up at the ceiling and shakes her head. "I knew the whole thing wasn't a good idea."

She seems to be talking to herself but then she looks back at me. "Kylie, being sensitive isn't a crime. And it doesn't mean you're immature. I didn't know exactly how this experiment of yours was going to turn out but I know there are some things it is best to learn for yourself." She gives a little laugh. "And I *thought* you might find out what maturity really means."

Whatever Momma wanted me to figure out on my own, I'm almost positive that I missed it. And the key problem is still there. "But what if my friends . . . leave me behind?"

"You and your friends have an awful lot of growing up ahead of you. Probably one of you is always going to be a little ahead or a little behind. And who that is will change with the wind. But I think all of you can handle a tear here and there. Okay?"

I nod. "Momma . . ." I start but then have to take a couple of gulps. "Do *you* think I'm ready for seventh grade?" She's a scientist. She believes in facts.

Momma grins big at me. "Are you kidding?" she asks. And then she pulls me into another hug. "Of *course* I do."

And in that moment, I don't really care that my experiment didn't work out like I wanted. And that feels . . . pretty mature.

Later, when I'm in my room and putting my picture for So You Wanna Be on my nightstand, I look at the seven of us smiling at the camera. Six rock stars and one glittery mermaid with big glamorous curls. I was so scared when I didn't go along with everybody. I thought for sure I would just burst into tears but . . . thinking for myself actually felt good. It felt grown.

I touch my hair; it feels soft, like those fuzzy socks I get every Christmas. Poofy can also be pretty. Melissa made me stand a little separate from them since I was dressed differently than everyone, but I didn't care one bit. I smiled big for the picture even though I was sure it meant my experiment had failed.

But then it hits me. My experiment *wasn't* a failure. My hypothesis was just wrong.

Doing what everybody else is doing doesn't make you more mature after all. Maybe it's really the opposite. I don't think I will say that to Momma because she will be way too pleased that I figured out she was right about independent thinking.

There's a knock on my door.

"Who is it?" I say.

A small voice says, "Brianna Stanton."

"Come in, Brianna Stanton."

Brianna slowly walks into my room. She lets out a small gasp of air. "You look beautiful, Kylie," she says.

"Oh, I'm sorry, Your Royal Highness," I say, bowing low. "I thought you said, *Brianna Stanton*. How couldn't I have recognized the lovely voice of my sister, Luna Sparkle?"

Brianna giggles, and then her face gets solemn. "Come quick, Lena," she says, her voice low and mysterious. "An evil sorcerer is in the kitch—" She pauses, and her forehead crinkles. "Is in the *cavern* making a horrible potion! We have to stop her!" She turns and runs out of my room.

I slide my seashell headband off and put it next to the picture. Then I race after my sister.

OBSERVATIONS

> Doing what everyone else does doesn't mean I shouldn't also think for myself.
> I observed something really bad today.
> I guess my experiment is over.

A Very True Thing

The next day Mara texts me early in the morning.

I've been texting Naomi over and over and she hasn't answered. Have you heard from her?

No, I text back. **She probably got her phone taken away. She'll get it back soon. She always does.** I don't text that I am not worried about when Naomi will have her phone back because I don't plan on texting her anytime soon. I don't know what I would say. I want to be a good friend but I am not sure if Naomi has been a very good friend to me.

Momma calls for me to come eat breakfast, so I text **Gotta go!** and put my phone away. It is strange not having our usual Oreo friendship.

Momma tells me at breakfast that she is taking me over to Naomi's once I finish eating and I almost choke on my oatmeal.

"Huh?" I ask. "But isn't she on punishment?"

"Naomi got in trouble?" Brianna sounds worried. Her eyes are wide and she has a spot of milk on her chin. "Why?" she asks. "What did she do?" Brianna loves all my friends but Naomi is her favorite. Probably because they both like to pretend all the time.

"Wipe your face," I tell her in a not nice voice, and hand her a napkin.

"Kylie," Momma warns.

"*Please,* wipe your face," I say but it still comes out a little grumpy. I am not mad at Brianna. But Naomi should not get to have friends over. If I had done something really bad, Momma wouldn't let me hang out with a friend. That seems like a reward.

Brianna cleans off her face and then balls up the napkin. "Good girl," she says, petting the crumpled wad like it's a pet. Then she puts it in her lap. "You're a very good girl," she whispers to it.

"You ready?" Momma asks me as she gets up from the table. "It's not going to be a long visit. I have a meeting with my adviser in a little while and you'll need to watch Brianna."

Usually, I would complain about not getting to

spend more time with one of my friends but I just say, "Fine."

In the car, Momma uses her thumb to turn down the music and I feel like I'm about to get a lecture. "Kylie," she says. "I know you're mad at your friend and maybe you have every right to be." She pauses and I can tell there is a "but" coming.

And big shocker, that is the next thing that comes out of Momma's mouth. "But," she says, "part of growing up means spending a lot of time being confused about *so* many things. And maybe most confusing of all is being unsure about how we feel about ourselves."

"I guess," I mumble, not sure what point Momma is trying to make. I see her eyes flick to the rearview mirror to check on Brianna.

Brianna isn't paying a bit of attention to us. She is humming to her new napkin "pet." Brianna's imagination is as big as Naomi's. I wonder if people who pretend all sorts of things have an easier time lying.

"You and Naomi just may have more in common than you think," Momma says.

"I don't steal," I say angrily.

"I know, Ky," Momma says. Then she sighs. "People react to things differently. And sometimes they don't make the best choices."

What does that have to do with me? I want to ask.

When we pull up in front of Naomi's house, I don't want to get out of the car.

"What am I supposed to say?" I ask Momma.

"Maybe," Momma says, "all you have to do is listen." She pats my knee encouragingly, but I don't even unfasten my seat belt. "While you and Naomi chat, Brianna and I are going to run to Local."

"Cookie! Cookie! Cookie!" Brianna shouts.

The Local is a coffee shop that Momma likes to go to when she is stressed about school. She says a cappuccino from there makes everything fall into place. And Brianna and I love their cookies. "No fair," I say. "I want a cookie."

"We will get you one," Momma says. "Now scoot."

As I walk to the front door, I think about what Momma said. I am sort of confused about myself. I had convinced myself that I had proven I was really grown-up and mature even though my hypothesis was false. But feeling this way about a friend, being mad at them when they're going through something rough doesn't feel mature at all. Maybe I'll never figure this out. I push the bell and the door opens immediately, as if Naomi had been standing there waiting for me.

"Hey," she says. She looks . . . scared. Like she knows I might not be happy to see her. In my phone there is a text to her that I haven't sent. It's an angry text message. I should delete it before I accidentally send it. I don't want to be angry at Naomi.

And I do not like seeing her look this way.

I like when she is being a *silly* tease and telling the best stories and making me laugh hard enough to cry happy tears—which taste sweeter than sad ones.

That is who Naomi *really* is. And that's the Naomi I want to see. I cross my eyes at her and stick out my tongue. She snort laughs and has to cover her mouth to keep any more snorts from coming out.

I don't turn to look, but I hear the *toot toot* of Momma's horn and the sound of her car pulling away. And Naomi takes a step back so I can come in. There's still a lot of boxes in the living room, but now some of them are taped closed. I pretend I don't notice as I follow Naomi to her room.

I'm shocked to see boxes in there. "You *are* moving?" I feel like I have been tricked. Was this why Momma made me come over? To find out one of my best friends is *leaving*?

But Naomi shakes her head, making her hair swoosh back and forth. "No, my dad wants me to have some of my stuff at his . . . his new place. Once he finds one."

I plop on her bed the way I have done a million

times and look around the room while I try to think of what to talk about.

Naomi sits next to me and slides her feet back and forth. Then she takes a big breath. "I'm sorry," she says.

I know she is apologizing for a whole lot of things. "It's okay," I say, trying to mean it. "I'm sorry about your parents," I add. "But it will be okay. *You* will be okay." I don't know this for sure, but Naomi is tough, or at least good at *acting* tough and sometimes that is good enough.

Naomi falls back on the bed and stares up at the ceiling. "Do you ever feel that you can't have the thing you really want?" She sounds so sad and I'm sure she isn't thinking about sunglasses or headbands.

"Yeah," I say slowly. "But, you can't . . ." I don't want to say it out loud but Naomi gets up on an elbow and looks me right in the face.

"Steal," she says, saying the word I couldn't. "I know. Both my parents were *so* mad at me. It's the first thing they've agreed on in like forever." She smiles ruefully. "I won't be doing anything like that again."

"Well *that's* a relief," I say. "Glad you're not planning a life of crime." Then I laugh so she knows I'm just kidding around.

"Yeah, that is one less thing you need to worry

about," Naomi says.

It feels like we're getting back to a good place, but something is still bothering me and I have to ask her about it.

"When I saw . . . I mean . . . Why did . . ." I squeeze my lips shut, not sure how to ask what I want to.

Naomi looks confused for a minute but then her mouth tightens as if it was just sewn shut and I'm sure she knows what I was going to ask. She sits back up and takes a deep breath. "You want to know about . . . about kissing Cory?" Her voice is so low I have to bend forward to hear her.

"Mm-hmm," I say just as low. She looks embarrassed and for some reason, I feel embarrassed too.

"I . . . I . . ." She twists her hands together and her head drops down making her hair fall in front of her face. I wait. Finally, she straightens up and faces me. She gives me a lopsided smile. "I'm sorry I lied. As soon as we kissed I wished we hadn't. And I thought maybe I could sort of pretend it didn't happen?"

I still don't understand. "But why?" I ask.

"The thing is . . . I thought I was ready to move on to the next thing," she says. "Seventh grade and being, you know, *grown* and everything." She smiles a little but her eyes aren't happy. "But . . ." She pulls her hair up like she's going to wrap it into a bun but then just lets it fall back to her shoulders. "What if I grow up too fast and you all don't want to be friends anymore?"

I'm shocked. *Naomi* has doubts? Momma was right about us being more alike than I realized. "I've been worried too," I admit. And suddenly I feel the familiar caterpillar in my nose, but this time, it doesn't worry me.

"What if middle school is awful?" Naomi asks in a low worried voice. "What if the eighth graders treat us like babies?"

Knowing my friend is scared about the future too makes the caterpillar disappear, and I sit up straighter. "Who cares?" I ask, and shrug. "*We* know we aren't babies." It feels like a very true thing. Something Mara would've said instead of me.

"Bet," Naomi says and grins.

"Will you do me a solid?" I ask, and Naomi nods without even asking me what it is. "Always tell each other the truth?"

"Dutely, *tutely,*" she says and sticks out her hand.

It feels like we have been waiting at a raised drawbridge and at last it came down for us to cross.

We shake on the solid but then I give her a hug and she hugs me back so tight it's like I'm being squeezed by a boa constrictor . . . and it feels great.

When we get home, Momma goes into her office and closes the door so she can meet with her adviser online.

I go into the backyard to work on my kata. I try Mr. Kim's advice of just letting my brain relax. But my brain is a bear trap trying to catch butterflies. I keep thinking I'm getting close to a good idea, but then my brain snaps pointy jaws down way too hard and the idea flutters away.

Brianna watches me from the under the shade of our magnolia tree. She is painting rocks with old fingernail polish of Momma's. Every once in a while she will shout a suggestion about adding more spins or how I should roll around on the ground like a roly-poly bug. "Do you want some of my magic rocks to throw at your opponent?" she asks.

Her suggestion catches me off guard and is so ridiculous that it makes me crack up. I guess that's just what my brain needed because suddenly the ideas that have been impossible to catch start to settle down, landing softly all around me.

"You are one smart cookie, Bree," I say.

"I know that already," she says and goes back to painting rocks.

ADDITIONAL OBSERVATIONS

- Maybe being (a little) immature is the best way to have great ideas.
- Nobody is just one thing or exactly who you think they are.
- Brains are strange and sometimes do not cooperate until you stop trying to make them.
- I think maybe me and my friends are actually close to being at the same level of maturity. Almost. I might even be a little bit more mature than Naomi. I'm sure she would not agree.

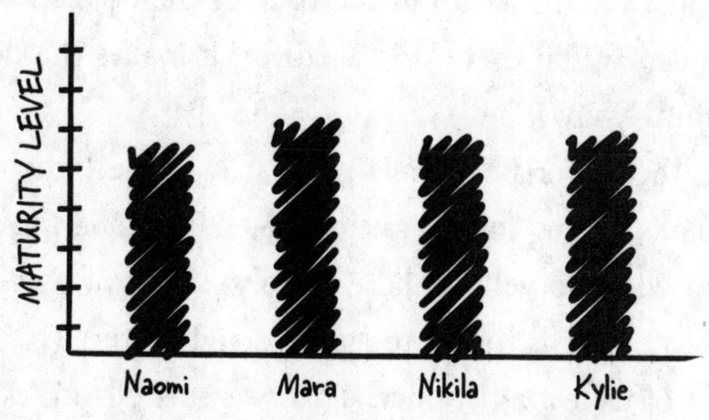

Warrior Spirit

Testing for the next belt level is a big production. Chairs are set up in the back of the dojo so parents can watch their kids perform. It makes the dojo extremely crowded.

At the lower belt levels there is a whole bunch of students testing for the same thing. Like when I tested from white to yellow there were so many of us, they had to break us into three groups and there were still eight of us testing at once. That was sort of fun, especially since it was a pretty easy test. But the higher you go, the fewer students are with you . . . and the tests get way harder.

Although there are many students testing today, I'm the only one testing for advanced brown. Maybe that's better. There isn't another student the sensei can compare me to that might be doing a better job. Still my stomach feels like it's full of fighting squirrels.

The gym is so noisy I can't hear the whiny old air conditioner. Maybe it's not even on. The dojo feels way too hot and sticky and smells like overripe bananas. I'm sitting crisscross apple sauce on the floor with all the other students waiting to test. The mat is cool on my bare feet, and I wipe my sweaty palms on the pants of my gi. I like that we wear black. Most dojos have their students wear white ones, but black looks tougher. At competitions we always stand out.

The group of students testing for their orange belt has finished. Mr. Kane calls each one's name and if they passed the test, he hands them their orange belt. You know you didn't pass if you just get a handshake. I know what that feels like. It feels like a hard pinch right on the tender part of your arm. I'm worried I'll get only a handshake today. I know I have my forms and kicks and bo staff routine down, but this will be the first time Mr. Kim sees my original kata. I've been working on it in secret so I can surprise him at how good it is . . . or maybe to keep him from seeing how bad it is.

I performed it for Momma and Dad last night and they clapped and said I would "definitely" pass my test today. But neither of them are karate experts so I can't really trust their opinion.

Dad being able to attend my test makes me feel like I have won the big, huge teddy bear prize at the fair. It totally makes up for him missing the promotion.

Mara sent me a text earlier saying **You got this!** And then a whole bunch of strong arm emojis. Even though she used the group chat, I know that it is only her and me reading the texts. Nikila still doesn't have her phone back and like I thought would happen, Naomi got hers taken away too. I haven't talked to her since that day at her house.

Momma told me that Audrey sent Naomi to her cousins for a little while so she didn't have to be around while her dad packed up and moved out. That was weeks ago.

I feel bad for Naomi. If my dad moved away and wasn't going to live with us anymore, I would need pages and pages of cry boxes to check off.

Even just thinking about it makes my chest feel tight and my stomach does an uncomfortable flip. I take a gulp of air but that doesn't help and I'm wondering if I have time to run to the bathroom before I'm called for my test when I see them.

Mara, Nikila, and Naomi.

I can't believe they are here! Nikila waves frantically at me and Mara rubs her hands together and grins and I can tell by the sneaky look on her face that she knew about this surprise. Naomi smiles but it's not her usual big wide grin.

"Kylie Stanton," Mr. Kim calls out and I get up without missing a beat.

I hear Brianna call out, "Go, Kylie!"

I bow low to Mr. Kim, and he bows back.

During the test, different sensei shout out the katas they want to see. As I move through them, I think of all the things Mr. Kim told me about concentration and strength and balance and breath. He told me I must be a spirit warrior. Strong and true.

In my bo staff routine, when I get to the part where I twirl the staff over my head like a helicopter, I don't even have to think about what my hands are doing because they know. I do one last hard strike at the end, and I hear applause and my dad saying, "She did that thing!" I'm breathing hard and feel tired, but I have one more thing to do.

My original kata.

I'm ready. I am Lena Sparkle, and I will defend my

twin Luna against the evil Seebatch. He stands no chance.

My kicks are hard and strong, and my strikes would knock a grown man down. As I go through the form, my eyes water and tears start dribbling down my face. I know exactly what type of tears they are. These are proud tears.

My last move is a stomp on the ground that would make Seebatch groan in agony. My chest is moving up and down like a trampoline with way too many kids jumping. But I manage to calm my breathing as I bow to Mr. Kim.

His face doesn't give anything away. He just nods and then joins the other sensei.

They all huddle and the dojo goes quiet except for their low murmuring. When Mr. Kim turns away from the group, he is holding an advanced brown belt.

I did it!

He calls me forward and bows and then he places the belt in my open hands. I want to jump up and down and yell, but I just bow back and then shake all the sensei's hands.

It's the mature thing to do.

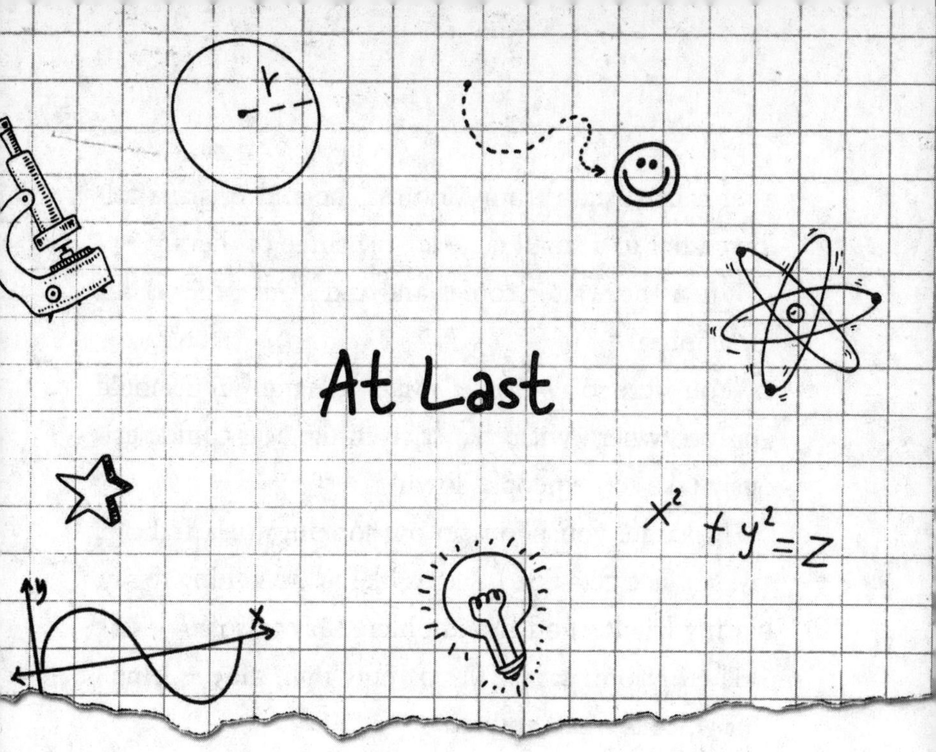

At Last

Finally, I'm having my sushi dinner. I feel like I had to wait way too long for this deliciousness. And Momma has worked some serious sparkle magic because somehow, she not only convinced Naomi's and Nikila's moms to let them come to my test, but also to go out for dinner after, so they get to have sushi too.

I guess she knew how much I missed my friends and how badly I'd want them around whether I passed the test or not.

When we got to the restaurant, Mom said, "Rob, why don't we let the girls sit at a table by themselves?"

Dad, of course, had all sorts of jokes about it, but

after a hard stare from Momma, he and Brianna followed her to a small table for the three of them.

When the waiter comes and takes our order, I ask for a Sprite.

"You were so awesome!" Mara tells me. "You should go everywhere with that stick thing. You could seriously take some people down!"

"In karate you never go out looking for a fight," I say. My face gets hot. It seems like a dorky thing to say, but my friends nod like I'm incredibly wise.

Then Naomi says, "My parents fight all the time." Her voice is small and sad.

"Maybe—" Mara says but then she stops.

"What?" Naomi asks.

"It's just that . . ." Mara pokes her chopsticks into the seaweed salad and swirls it around. "Maybe it's better then? For them to break up? Like it must be sort of awful to be fighting so much?"

"I just don't see why they couldn't get along! It's like they didn't care what I wanted," Naomi says. "And everything is going to be different."

I reach across the table and grab Naomi's hand. "Not everything," I say. "*We* won't be different."

Mara grins and says, "Yep, we'll still be large and in charge. And if people don't like it?" She shakes her fist.

"Knuckle sandwich!"

"Yes!" Nikila shouts and pounds her fist on the table.

Momma glances over at us and frowns.

"Nik!" I say. "Grow up! We're *seventh* graders!"

Nikila just laughs. She knows I'm only teasing. Then she gives me a sneaky smile and puts way too much wasabi on her piece of sushi. "Ack!" she cries and holds her nose to try to stop the burn.

"Thought you liked spicy," I tease.

"That's a whole different thing," she says and takes a few gulps of water.

I put a *reasonable* amount of wasabi on a piece of dragon roll and put the whole thing in my mouth. It tastes better than ever.

Naomi clears her throat and we all look at her. "That day at the beach," she starts. She shifts around and looks uncomfortable like someone snuck a pin on her seat.

Mara and Nikila both get still as if they have turned into prairie dogs.

"Kylie was telling the truth," Naomi says. "About . . . you know . . ."

Mara sits back in her seat with a satisfied look on her face. It is an I-knew-it! look.

"Why didn't you want us to know?" Nikila asks.

Then she adds in a whisper, "Was it nasty?"

"No, but—" Naomi starts, and she looks at me with a pleading expression.

"It's okay," I quickly say. I'm grateful that she told Nikila and Mara the truth, but now I want it behind us, just like Naomi does. "You don't have to tell us the details." I give Mara and Nikila stern looks. "Some things can be *private*. *Everybody* knows that."

Naomi sighs gratefully and Mara raises her hands like she's saying "What did I do?"

Then Naomi looks over both her shoulders like she's checking for spies, and leans toward me, her hands clutching the edge of the table. "Hey, Kylie," she whispers.

I feel a little flutter in my chest. I don't know what she is going to say but I lean forward too.

"It's *obvious* that you are secretly a ninja," Naomi says. "Killer assassin! I can't believe you have kept it secret this long." Making her voice even quieter, she asks, "When is your next mission?"

Nikila giggles. "She is totally a ninja!"

"Teach me some ninja dance moves!" Mara says and gets up and starts shaking her hips from side to side.

She looks so ridiculous I can't help cracking up and suddenly, all of us are laughing so hard that tears pour down our faces. I'm sure everyone in the restaurant thinks we are completely immature, but you know what? I don't care.

When I get home that night, I hang my advanced brown belt on the hook behind my door. All my karate belts hang there together in a rainbow. All that is missing is red and black. I'll get those too one day.

I pull out my science notebook and go through it all.

Reading all my observations makes me feel strange. Sort of proud. Sort of silly. What does it mean?

It takes some heavy-duty thinking, but I'm able to complete my experiment like a real scientist.

CONCLUSION

> My hypothesis was not correct.
> It was based on a faulty assumption, but I am still glad I did my experiment because now I know that crying a lot (like a lot a lot) ≠ being immature.

Writing that is like a kick to the head. My experiment sure did teach me an awful lot about what is and isn't mature.

> Best friends can be different in a bunch of ways and still stay friends forever.

I smile at that last fact. My friends and I do have a lot of differences, but I think we're alike in the ways that really matter. I'm so glad I'll have them with me to face all the changes of seventh grade.

"Se-venth grade. Se-venth grade," I quietly chant. And then I can't help but add one more important conclusion.

> Mermaids are 1000% better than rock stars.

Acknowledgments

For a book that centers so much on crying, it sure did bring me a lot of joy to tell Kylie's story. Maybe because I had such awesome support all along the way. I so appreciate my agent Brenda's honesty and astuteness, and my amazing editor, Alessandra, who is so patient and kind and whip-smart. Big thanks to all my writer friends who allow me to bug them on the regular (especially Jenn, Gillian, Mariama, Jasmine, Rebecca, Sabaa, Alicia, and Keely). I am part of a wonderful Bay Area writing community that offers advice, support, laughter, and food, and I'm so happy to have you all in my life. Special shout-out to Sally and Lydia who gave such great insightful notes. Thank you to my colleagues at the day job who are incredibly supportive and cheer me on and especially my plank crew (Courtney, Janet, Alice, and Patricia). Thank you to Yesha for the read—so appreciate it!

There are a ton of publishing folks behind the scenes who do all the hard work of getting a book out in the world (I see you, Caitlin!) and I'm forever grateful to the team at HarperCollins who do so much heavy lifting to get books into the hands of readers (especially the copy editors—I'd look like such a ninny without them). And thanks so much to Aly and Karina for their work in getting us over the finish line!

And this cover y'all! What?! Isn't it gorgeous? Cleverly designed by David DeWitt and gorgeously illustrated by Brittany Bond, it's perfect. I love it so much.

Thank you to my SOTYs (Marisa, Lisa, Lisa, Kelli, Kim, and Dawn) and my dear friends Griff, Alice, Trudy, and Terrie. I need each and every one of you! Thank you to my amazing family. My Mamasita Baunita, Jimmy, Pam, Linda, all my true family in-laws, my aunties and uncles, nieces, nephews, cousins . . . we are mighty, wild, and strong (and highly ridiculous, which I adore). I will never run out of stories with all of you in my life.

Big love and thanks to Jordan, Morgan, and my forever love, Keith. You are everything.

And thank you, readers, for allowing me to tell you one more story.